I0739379

1916-*ish*

EBONY McKENNA

Copyright

The moral right of Ebony McKenna to be identified as the author of this work has been asserted by her in accordance with the Copyright, Designs and Patents Act, 1988. All rights reserved. This book is sold subject to the condition that is shall not, by way of trade or otherwise be lent, resold, hired out or otherwise circulated without the author's prior consent.

Third edition, 2016

First published by Ebony McKenna, 2015
Text copyright Ebony McKenna, 2015
Cover design The Masked Maven, 2015
ISBN 978-0-9953839-0-6
Printed and bound in Australia by Blurb

Author's note

While many of the events described in this novel are historically accurate to the best of the author's knowledge, many more are fictional events created by the author. All characters are fictional and bear no resemblance to real people, alive or dead, whether in this world or any presently-explored alternate reality.

– ONE –

THESE blue woollen pants are so itchy they may as well be made from steel wool. Every step I take scrapes my skin. Bet I break out in a rash. Stupid skin. Stupid over-sensitive, magnet-for-allergies skin.

It won't do any good to scratch. But it will feel so good. Quick check, nobody's watching. If I can time my step right and rub it just like . . . ah!

We squeeze past another group of men standing in this clay-walled trench, looking like soldiers. They are soldiers. I mean, soldiers from World War One. Pretending to be, at any rate. We're here for a re-enactment to celebrate the centenary of something called *the Battle of the Sum* and all I can think about is how much I want to scratch my thigh.

This re-enactment is all about being authentic, so my horizon blue wool trousers are made of real wool.

I *know*!

Just thinking about how much I itch is making everything else itch. I can't scratch my head because I have a helmet on and all my crazy ginger hair is smooshed up inside it. That's right, I'm ginger. Deal with it.

If I take the helmet off, I'll never get my hair back in there.

Maybe Marianne can help me scratch this itch? Maybe she's just as itchy? We could scratch each other's backs. Oh, that spot just between my shoulder blades that I can never reach and which is burning now.

Marianne's walking ahead of me, marching along. The trenches are built like a hedge maze, only made of mud instead of . . . hedges I guess. We're doing this experience together, along with her brother Luc.

Wow, a whole couple of minutes without thinking about Luc. I swear I am getting better at trying to ignore him.

The rifle on my shoulder weighs a tonne. If we could just stop walking for a moment I could lean it down here against the wall and stretch out my shoulder.

Marianne turns back and gives me a look that could be sympathy and says in her gorgeous French accent, 'We will be in place soon, Ingrid. A bit of running. A bit of mud. Then tomorrow we spend the day at a spa.'

I'm looking forward to that massage and facial tomorrow as I shift the heavy rifle on my shoulder. Why is this weapon so heavy? Probably made of lead. Probably giving me lead poisoning just by holding it.

I can't help it. I'm going to have to sneak another ogle at Luc, who is a few paces ahead of Marianne. Never thought I'd go for the 'man in uniform' look but in this case I'll make an exception. He turns me into a mental case just thinking about him. And I'm supposed to treat him like a brother? Ha!

It's my own stupid fault for reading *Anna and the French Kiss* before I boarded the plane.

Have I taken my Ritalin this morning?

Marianne and Luc are my sister and brother while I'm here on exchange. Would I follow my real brother, if I had one, into battle? Hell to the no! I don't even follow Dad into the mock battles he signs up for back home, when he and his mates bring the Eureka Stockade back to life. He would love this so hard. Can't wait to tell him all about it.

I'm no history nerd. I'm simply embracing a cultural experience walking through these genuine trenches from history. History is culture. The best way to learn about culture is to fully embrace it, right? That's what Luc had said. Or maybe Marianne had said it. OK someone said it and I agreed to it. Luc and Marianne wanted to be here and who am I to be the handbrake?

I remember learning something about World War One at school. All about the ANZAC spirit and mateship. But that was all about a place called Gallipoli, and I don't think that's anywhere around here. I don't remember learning about this battle we're doing. Luc said it was one of the biggest and bloodiest messes of the war. They should have taught us that at school, right? Maybe they did and I was looking out the window.

Why do schools have windows if they don't want us to look out?

What was I? Oh yeah. We're bringing the war back all of it in sanitised detail. A few hundred cosplay geeks in a field.

Here's something you don't learn in a history book: the smell. The clay here is definitely not the same as the stuff I'm used to handling in the school art room. It's mouldy. Like wet compost and sewage. The sooner I'm out of this trench the better.

We've reached the end of the standing soldiers, there's a space here so we stop marching and take our positions. Finally, I can rest the rifle and scratch my thigh.

Bliss!

'*Revue!*' a man calls out from further down. He's a big stretch of a bloke, looks like he's been ducking under doorways from age twelve. The beacon-red cap on his head makes him the perfect target. Is it authentic? I'll look it up when we get home. A bright red cap on such a tall man would be suicide in a real war.

Maybe people weren't so tall in the olden days?

He's talking too fast. Time for my default-confused face and Marianne translates for me. 'Inspection time, he wants to make sure the guns are not loaded. It's the only difference between this and the real thing.'

'Keeping it real.' I can't help giggling. This is maximum surreal. There was one of those old-time aeroplanes parked in the field when we arrived. It looked like a death trap.

'Shhh.' Luc looks our way and gives us a frown to share. 'Be serious.'

Whenever someone tells me off, I feel a bit sick. I hate being told off. Some days I feel like all I do is get told off. I don't even need to know the language, the tone is enough.

Oh man, what is that smell? Are people smoking? Probably authentic nineteen-sixteen cancer sticks judging from the caustic stench. Just one more thing I hadn't counted on in my exchange visit–so many people in France smoke! LOL! Exploding irony gland, two of the smokers have gas masks hanging around their necks.

I can't help shaking my head at a stray thought. Mum gave me 'the talk' before I left home for France. Home for me is Melbourne, Australia. I should miss it more. I really should. Top of my parents' fears for me coming here were horny French boys. That went double for my host family. 'No matter how good-looking he is, you must treat Luc like a brother,' Mum had told me. They also made me to promise not to smoke. The first of their fears has taken care of itself; Luc isn't the slightest bit interested in me. The smokers on the other hand are impossible to avoid. What do they put in those reekful cigarettes? Tarmac?

The officer in his distinctive red cap inspects Luc's weapon, then inserts a rubber bayonet on the tip.

'How come you're allowed to have a fake blade and we're not allowed to wear jeans?' Jeans are my new idea of freedom. Has anyone noticed me scratching about? If I move my knee this way just a little . . . ah, so much better.

Luc rolls his eyes. So help me, I can't help noticing how they glint gold and green in the sunlight. He and Marianne have the same sort of eyes and dusty brown hair. Not usually the combination I go for. I love the Henry Cavill super dark hair and blue eyes, but there's something about Luc that makes my brain stammer.

'We are trying to be as authentic as possible,' Luc says. 'You cannot wear denim because the soldiers didn't.' Then Luc translates the exchange for the 'red cap'.

Authentic with a fair whack of fudging. Marianne and I both have long hair, but we've twisted it under our helmets to make us look more like boys. Swear to God, I am the least convincing boy in the universe judging by how tightly these pants fit across my very girly round arse. 'Are we getting fleas next?'

Luc and the officer glare at me. There's that twist of guilt in my stomach. Why can't I keep my mouth shut?

The officer barks more orders in French and for the life of me I have no idea what he says. Time to hand over the Get Out Of Jail Free card.

'Je suis Australien.' I never tell anyone I'm British. Not that I'm lying when I say I'm Australian. I was born in Melbourne, so I'm totally Aussie. But Dad's from Caerphilly and Mum's from Bristol, so I could go either way. But it's always better to say you're Australian when

you're in France. Smoothes things over. Which is totally dumb because the French and the Brits were on the same side in both world wars.

I *know*!

'*Merveilleux!*' Red-cap-man gives me a smile and launches into a speech I don't have a hope of understanding. He thumps me on the shoulder and says in English, 'Enjoy your history,' before moving on to the next group of soldiers.

'What did he say?'

Luc gives me his fresh-out-of-braces grin, which gives me more of those not-very-sisterly thoughts. 'He said his grandfather met many Australian soldiers. They were the bravest men on earth, next to us, of course. Now get ready, we go over the top in a few minutes. Don't be scared, I'll take care of you.'

I must remember Luc is my brother. I must remember Luc is my brother.

Oh wow, look at those birds. They're flying in 'V' formation, mimicking the bombers that will fill the skies in the war after this one.

I don't think I did take my Ritalin.

So many Australians died in that war too, the one they made all the movies about.

Every time the sun comes out behind the clouds, it burns my head. The helmet conducts so much heat. Might not do much running after all. Might have a sip of water and take it easy. Ugh! The water is tainted. As much as I want the complete nineteen-sixteen soldier experience, a case of gastro is not on my list.

'So, how do I fire this thing?' I turn to Luc for instruction. He might show me how to hold it, maybe wrap his arms around my shoulders to demonstrate. Maybe a reprise of that moment a few days after I arrived when he suggested we use 'tu' instead of 'vous' and he looked at me so sweetly I could hardly breathe.

LOL, siblings. Luke and Leia much?

No such luck. Luc smiles but stands his ground. 'It does not matter. You will not be firing it. Go one hundred meters and fall down. Play dead. The field ambulance will come and get you.' Just as a brother might explain to his sister.

Mum has nothing to worry about on the randy French boys front.

'Isn't this exciting?' Marianne says, 'Much better than learning from a book.'

'Yes and no. It's mad exciting. But my feet are killing me. These pants are so itchy. Goddammit it's driving me nuts.'

Luc gives me an unreadable look.

Something lurches in my belly.

A booming voice yells out something in French. Everyone around me stands to attention. Troops stomp down the trenches carrying wooden ladders that reach all the way to the top of the mud and timber walls. So that's how we're getting out!

Shrill whistles fill the air and bounce inside my head. Luc grabs the ladder and scrambles to the top, roaring a war cry.

Everyone is yelling and hollering. It's contagious. Marianne gives me a salute and follows her brother. Her high-pitched girlie squeal is so out of place with all the deep male voices.

My turn now. I grab the ladder and immediately get a splinter. Pulling my hand back and sucking on it, a sweet, rusty taste fills my mouth.

A taste for blood.

I'm a soldier!

With a primal scream coming all the way from my boots, I scale the ladder and leap out onto the field. The sun is shining something glorious.

The ground is lumpy, my knees and ankles beg for mercy already. Oh great, my hair has come loose and the plait is thumping against my shoulders. No time to fix it, I'll keep running.

Jogging, really.

In fact I might walk now because I'm puffed already and my tired legs have turned to wood.

The sound of men baying for blood fills my ears. Over to one side, a whole group of them have fallen down dead in unison. They make it look so believable.

'Death to the enemy!' Reckless enthusiasm fills me and I break into a jog again. Not enough to catch up with Luc and Marianne who are out in front. Nope, I have to walk again because I'm getting a cramp. Might play dead in a minute just so I can get my breath back. I am so not fit.

Shlock! My foot lands on soft ground and I overbalance. Don't you hate that feeling like you're falling over? You've got a pico-second to get your balance back or you're in for a world of pain.

Why is it raining now? The sun was out a moment ago. Huh, I guess Melbourne isn't the only place with four seasons in one day.

Luc and Marianne turn around, confusion all over their faces. They jog back to me but they're moving in slow-time.

'Did you feel that?' Luc asks.

I have no idea what he means. Chunks of mud and clay are flying everywhere.

What is that reverberating noise? It's a what? Someone is flying that plane? How did they even get it off the ground?

Soldiers' screams are louder. Coldness seeps through me. Rain hammers wet bullets onto my head. Dank mud and decay burns my nostrils.

'We're going back,' Marianne says. 'We can start again when the weather clears.'

Luc and Marianne step closer to me. That plane comes in low overhead and we throw ourselves to the ground in panic.

A blink later they're gone.

The world falls away.

Sharp burning pain rips through my leg. A guttural scream leaps out my throat. I'm too scared to look at my leg in case I've done something stupid. It feels broken but I haven't even moved.

Why am I falling?

Face-first into mud. The uniform is probably ruined but I don't care. The smell is so gag-worthy, I have to breathe through my mouth.

Don't look at your leg. Don't look at your leg.

Stupid twit, I look at my leg and can't breathe for the shock of it. Cherry red blood oozes over my calf. The wool pants unravel at the wound site, revealing an ugly, ripped gash across my skin. It's so painful I wish I could pass out, but I'm so cold and shivery I'm wide-awake. And the smell. Did I mention the smell?

The dumbest thing I could do right now? Get a closer look at it. Oh man, my leg is a mess!

There's barbed wire all over the ground around me. I didn't notice it before. Normally I can't help seeing everything all the time. Stupid wire. I must have gotten tangled in it or something. But the wound doesn't match the kind of jagged injury wire would cause. The mess on my leg is broad and flat and hurts like hell.

Is it a bullet wound? We're not supposed to be armed!

It's all feeling far too real. Cold muddy water soaks the uniform and seeps into my skin. My next stupid move is to splash the water over the wound. I just want to get a better look at it, OK?

Seriously bad idea. It stings like a bitch.

Ratatatatatatatatat! Headsplitting gunfire peppers the air. It sounds so real. Is it from the plane overhead?

Someone is screaming.

Like a mole, I bury myself into the mud. I'm flicking mud over my hair to hide it. I'll put up with the stink if it means I survive. Shivers stab my skin. A chill in my back, a frozen ache in my jaw. Cold head, cold arms, cold tummy. Except for the white-hot pain in my leg, I'm chilled all over. My only hope is to embrace the mud. If some nutjob out there has real ammo, I'm staying buried forever. Rain keeps falling, plastering the pants onto my skin. Sick misery spreads out from my belly. Mud leeches into my pores.

How the hell am I going to explain this to Mum and Dad?

– TWO –

BULLETS whiz and crack like fireworks. I'm staying lower than a worm. All around is the sound of people running then falling down hard. Moans carry on the wind. Someone collapses beside me and coats me with a new spray of mud.

Mud gushes out from this man's back. Oh God, It's not mud, it's blood. When he tries to breathe he makes gargled, bubbly noises. He's drowning on land.

It could so easily be me.

Or Luc.

Or Marianne. Yes, I should think of her too.

Nobody is stopping the idiot with the gun. It's not my heartbeat making all that noise. It's machine guns. Loads of them.

'Get down! The guns are loaded!' I scream out to anyone who will listen, hoping Luc and Marianne made it back to the trench before the world turned mad.

Why are there so many soldiers still marching around? They keep moving forward in formation. And they keep falling. Not like the way I thought they would. In the movies, they're all limbs arching in a graceful dance before falling in dramatic shapes. No. These men march forward then simply crumple mid-stride with a sickening sound of smashing bones and ripping flesh. Some of them try to get up, full of twitching and uncontrolled movements, only to fall again. And to think my parents thought France would be safer than America because of the campus killing sprees.

Another soldier falls into my crater splashing us both with mud.

How the hell do I get out of here?

He's whimpering. So I guess that means he's not dead, right?

'Are you OK?' I whisper to him.

He only sniffles; says something I can't understand. More crying-sniffles follow. He looks hungry-skinny, and his hair is greasy and stuck together. That could be from the rain pelting us, rather than not washing, I guess.

'Stay down low with me, we'll be OK.' If he doesn't get my words, I'm hoping he at least gets the 'I'm shitscared too' tone of my voice.

He mutters something like, 'lash' and says it over and over. With the crying. Poor bastard.

After what feels like an eternity, whistles blow in the air. The gunfire stops.

How long will it last?

Somebody grabs me by the foot. I'm screaming and kicking at their hands. 'No, you can't take me!'

It's two men, one has me by the legs, another has me under the armpits and they're carrying me. They are saying something in French and taking me away from the battlefield.

Oh thank God. They're rescuing me! That must mean someone has stopped the gunman for good. Relief has me sagging. Wait, the other guy in the mud pit. I fight the rescuers off and stagger-crawl back to the crying man in the crater and drag him out too. Then the four of us make a zig-zaggy run through the mud and barbed wire to safety.

We're back in a trench, I look about but can't recognise any faces. It's full of hipsters; we have reached maximum moustache. Was there another group of cosplayers next to ours maybe? These guys look even more authentic, what with the shaggy hair and mud all over them.

And the overripe smell of deodorant dodgers.

Since when were the walls around here so flimsy? They're ready to fall down with the next puff of wind. Chunks of broken timber stick out of the walls like shrapnel.

'Did you get him, the gunman?'

A sea of furrows, creased in confusion, look at me.

'*Je suis Australien.*' It's worth a shot.

'*Merde!*'

I know that one.

'Where is Luc?' Nobody wants to understand me. 'Luc Durand? Marianne Durand?'

'*Elle est une fille!*'

I know that one too. 'Of course I'm a girl! Where are my friends?'

A whistling sound fills the air. In the time it takes me to think how much it sounds like a bomb, there's a sickening bang somewhere up in the mud. The ground shakes. The air fills with clods of earth and bits of . . . Oh God, is that someone's hand?

A soldier runs screaming towards us. '*Grenade! Allons-y!*'

Lots of things happen at once. Someone grabs blankets and runs back down the trench. Two others grab me under the armpits and run off with me in the other direction.

A deafening boom takes out my ears and my stomach

falls through the floor.

***

I wake with a headache the size of Uluru and a blisteringly sore leg. This is an eerily quiet, cold room with creamy coloured walls made from stone. One high window lets a shaft of light in. A man on a crucifix is on the wall. He's staring at me.

Thorns in his forehead, blood on his hands and feet.

Bed is a hessian sack stretched across pieces of wood. The kind of thing Scouts make on camping weekends. Blinding pain smacks me inside the head when I try and sit up. Best to I lie down again. Muddy knots of hair stick into the back of my scalp. My stomach blurgles in hunger, the noise bouncing off the walls.

'Water.' My voice is husky.

Nuns. Three real, honest-to-God nuns wearing serious looking habits come in to the room and lean over me. I'm so not used to seeing Nuns. And they came in so quickly, like they must have been just outside, waiting for me to wake up. One of them pours me a drink into a really small glass and I wobble up onto one elbow to take it. Most of the water gets in my mouth. That's good, right?

Shifting positions in bed, fresh pain bursts through my leg. I remember the battlefield. The people falling down dead around me. The noise. The panic. The smell.

The nuns look so young and serene with thin, pale faces. They have no smell, which makes for a nice change. I haven't seen nuns since the time my art class back home visited that big church with the stained glass windows. There were nuns there that day, but they were little old prunes, not vibrant young women like the ones standing over me.

The shocks keep coming when one of them speaks and I understand every word. That blow to my head must have shaken something loose.

'Holy sh–I mean, awesome, I can understand you!' In my condition, I'm not making sense.

As one, the three sisters make a cross-motion over their chests. I cringe. Not a great start.

'You speak The Regent's English?' One of them says.

I don't know who the regent is, but it's English so I'm happy. And their English sounds better than mine, so we won't have to resort to sign language and Speaking. Really. Slowly. 'Yeah, I'm Australian. Sorry about swearing. Um, can I speak to Marianne and Luc?' See, I put Marianne first. For once. Luc's smiling face appears in my mind with a stab of regret. For no good reason either. He's barely paid me any attention since I arrived in France but I can't help liking him. I'm not even sure why. Is it because we're living together, or am I the kind of girl who velcro-bonds with the first boy who looks her way?

'They are not here,' one of the nuns says.

Not here because they are safe, or not here because . . . ? Dread clamps my heart. I can't stop thinking Luc and Marianne might be dead.

'I am Sister Augustine, this is Sister Paul and Sister Benedict.' The main nun says. 'Why were you disguised as a soldier?'

Aside from the fact they're speaking English and we're in France (where I always thought they hated the English), why do these women have boys' names?

I want to ask about Marianne and Luc, but the look on the nuns' faces compels me to answer their question. 'The clothes? Long story. They wanted it all to look real y'know? It was part of the anniversary or something, so .

. . Look, can you tell me if Luc and Marianne are OK? Someone started firing real bullets out on the battlefield and . . . hang on a minute, this is a hospital isn't it?' It doesn't look like any hospital I've ever seen. For a start, where are all the drips and beeping machines and gadgets? Everyone in hospital on TV has an oxygen tube under their nose. Speaking of TV, shouldn't there be one on the wall?

Do they know what medicine I should be on?

The nuns exchange glances before Sister Augustine speaks again. 'Every ward is full of men. It would not be decent for a maiden like yourself to be in there with them.'

A *maiden*? Who talks like that? My brain snags on an earlier phrase. 'Every ward? Jesus how many did the shooter get?'

Judging by the fresh exchange of confused looks and crossing motions, I'm not making myself very well understood. And yet we're both speaking the same language.

Go figure!

A bell tinkles in the distance. Sister Paul and Sister Benedict leave while Sister Augustine puts her palm to my forehead. A stern expression comes over her. 'What is your name, child, and how old are you?'

'Ingrid Calloway. I'm almost sixteen and I'm from Melbourne, Australia.'

Not a flicker of interest shows. 'Indeed? You have come a long way. Why do you dress as a man? A battlefield is no place for a maiden such as yourself.'

Finger-combing my hair, I catch a knuckle on a tangle. I pull my hand away and it's covered in nasty white powder.

The nun is displeased. 'All patients are treated for lice on admission. We run a clean hospital here.'

That's taking authenticity to a whole new level! 'It was just a re-enactment and stuff. It was supposed to be good fun. Learning about history.'

The nun turns on the disappointment and slam! I'm feeling the guilt even though I'm not Catholic.

'Stop pretending. I believe you are a spy. Has the *boche* run out of men that they must use girls for such hideous work?'

'A spy? What? I'm from *Australia*, not Austria!' So many people get them confused. Americans mostly. High time I got out of here. 'My leg feels so much better.' It's a lie, but worth a shot, 'If you could just bring me my bag, it's got my phone in it. I'll call my parents and let them know I'm OK. It must be all over the news by now. They'll be freaking out.' My fingers are twitching from my need to tweet.

Sister Augustine draws a long breath and looks as if she might be saying a silent prayer or ten. 'You were brought in as you are. You have no belongings. Despite your circumstances, we will not hand you over to the authorities for they would surely send you to the firing squad. We are children of God. We do not kill our fellow man or woman. You will stay here and work in the kitchen gardens until this horrible war is ended.' A smirk comes over Sister Augustine's face, 'One more thing. You are not a very good spy. With your fiery hair, you stand out too much.'

'Thanks . . .' I think. The pounding in my head begins again. Are the nuns part of the re-enactment, perhaps? In which case she's taking her role far too seriously. 'If you could tell me where the phone is that would be awesome. I feel fine now. I can get up and everything.'

To prove my point, I sit up and dangle my feet over the side of the bed. The pain is still there. My hair falls about my face and smells like dirt. Probably because it is full of dirt. And that white powder. I breathe hard and stand on my leg. It burns with pain but . . . I think this is doable.

'Whoa, where are my clothes?' They've got me in some kind of nightgowny sack.

'It is not decent for a maiden to wear men's clothes. We have supplied you with garments donated from the parish.'

'Ri-i-ght.'

Sister Augustine walks out and I use the private time to try walking on my bad leg. They've bandaged it so I can't see how it looks. When Sister comes back in, I'm walking up and down and each step feels worse yet better. It must have been a graze. Those ones that don't go deep but really, really hurt. Like that time I fell off my bike and skinned my hands. Took hours to pick the dirt and stones out of it.

The stack of folded clothes Sister gives me includes a long skirt and a stuffy button-up shirt. The bra looks like a strange tank-top with straps. Hilariously, the full-coverage underpants tie up at the sides with string. Sexy times!

Goosebumps spread over my skin so I dress quickly to combat the seeping chill. 'All done. Can you show me where the phone is?'

'Do you mean the telephone?'

My head thinks, 'well, duh!' but I hold it back and try a polite, 'Yes, thank you'.

Your parents are connected to the telephone?' Sister looks confused.

'Of course.'

Another strange look; another swirl of guilt in my belly. Why am I always getting into trouble for stuff I don't even do?

The guilt-sick gets worse when the nun leads me to a draughty room. On the wall is one of those classical paintings of a young girl with dark hair, combed flat against her head with lots of curls around her ears. She's wearing a white dress that looks like a shiny meringue. Underneath it, the words, '*The Regent Victoria*' are etched onto a gold plaque. She reminds me of the actress in that young Queen Victoria movie I saw. Was she ruler of France as well? Maybe they've just shoved the picture on the wall because it looks old?

On a side table is a thin metal object with cone-shaped bits attached to it. It's all joined together with a thick cable. 'That's the phone?' My leg is aching from the short walk so the words come out ruder than they should.

'Of course. We are becoming a modern convent. We had the telephone machine installed at the outbreak of the war. The doctor lets us know when we have more wounded soldiers coming.'

Outbreak of the war? Which one, the Napoleonic? 'It belongs in a museum!' It doesn't even have any numbers on it for dialling out. 'How does it work?'

'You lift the receiver and wait for the operator to answer. Then you tell her the name of the person you're calling.'

'Ri-i-ght.' For a second I wonder if the nun is playing a practical joke on me. I pick up the part of the phone that looks like a salt-shaker and hold it to my ear. There's no dial tone. Sister flicks the lever a few times. An operator's scratchy voice comes down the line. I give her my number in Melbourne and emphasize it's in Australia, not Austria.

The operator shouts at me. 'This is an important line. It is for emergencies only! Do not make stupid jokes when men are dying!'

Luc and Marianne. Are they dying?

'I'm not joking. I'm trying to let my parents know I'm OK because they'll be watching the news and freaking out about the shooting today.'

Click. The operator hangs up.

I can't even. Tears blob through my vision and I drop the phone. 'What the hell is going on?' Behind my ribs, my heart is hammering. It hurts to breathe. A strange fuzzy feeling spreads over my skin. I'm going to pass out. Only then do I remember I've sworn at a nun and it all becomes too much. 'I want my Mum!'

'Hush child, you have been foolish, but you have learned your lesson. Espionage is no game for children.'

'But I haven't done anything wrong!' Why is the nun being so stupid? 'Can you please try the phone again and tell the operator to put me through to my parents in Melbourne?'

The nun puts her hand on my forehead and makes a tisking sound. 'I will see what can be done about sending a telegram. Give me your parents' name and address.'

Fog swallows me. 'What's a telegram?'

One of the nuns I met earlier walks into the telephone room. 'Sister Augustine, we have a visitor at the main gate, a young man looking for his cousin. I believe he means this girl.'

'He's alive?'

Heat races up my neck. I hope he has Marianne with him. See, I can think of her. Sometimes.

– THREE –

ORANGE and red clouds streak the sky. So disorienting, it should be mid-afternoon but it's way later. The nuns walk beside me to the main gate. There's Luc, standing in his mud-spattered army uniform. When he smiles at me, I'm lighter on my feet. Even my leg doesn't ache as much.

Shock the first: He grabs me by the shoulders. He's so close his irises dilate. Shock the second: He kisses me on both cheeks and squishes me in a bear hug. He says something like, 'You are safe!' but my brain's already shut down.

So much has happened so fast I can't even process it. I don't get how Luc can be so nice to me right now when the rest of the time he ignores me.

We're still in the hug when I remember the third member of the family. 'Where's Mari? Is she . . ?' I don't want to finish the sentence. And another thing. How long do I keep this hug going for? It's the most lovely, warm hug, but if I hang on while he lets go, that's going to be all kinds of awkward. He also smells of sweat and dirt. It's not offensive or anything, but if he smells, I must be on the nose too. Especially with that nit powder in my hair.

'Mari is waiting for us,' he whispers, his grip loosening.

That's my cue to let go. What do I do with my hands

now? Oh look, the skirt the nuns gave me has pockets. Embarrassment makes me talk too much. 'I haven't been able to call my Mum yet. Do your parents know we're OK? It must be all over the news. As soon as we can get to an internet cafe I can let them know I'm all in one piece.' My friends back home will be having meltdowns for sure.

Luc leans in close, puts his mouth to my ear and for a second I'm hoping he's going to kiss me again. His voice is low. 'We have to get out of here. Right now.'

The distant rumble of something rolls through the air. Sick dread spreads out from my belly like ripples in a pond.

Luc pulls away from me and turns to the nuns. 'Thank you for looking after my cousin, holy sisters.' He presses his hands together in prayer and thanks. 'She has not been at all well. Our home suffered a direct hit from the *Boche* and she hasn't been the same since. Three times now she has dressed as a soldier and followed me to the trenches. I have been granted leave to take her to an institution.'

An institution? The insulting little . . . So much for thinking he might like me.

'My family thanks you for taking such good care of her.' Luc's hand grabs my wrist. With a swift tug, he marches me towards the street. The touch of his skin should be sending warm flurries through me, if it wasn't so harsh and grabby.

'Close the gate!' Sister Benedict orders.

'Run!' Luc yells. With a sudden jerk, he yanks me with him. Each step burns my bad leg but I keep pace, desperate to stay with him. Pain stabs my chest. The gates are half closed. Luc grabs the iron railing and hauls it back, sending a nun sprawling.

Whacking a nun is seriously bad karma but there's no

time to stop and think. Just run. Run down the cobblestone streets, around the corner, down a laneway. Ignore the burning in my leg. The pain in my chest. Just run.

Oh, look! A butterfly!

'Come on!' Luc growls.

And another thing. Cobblestones are mental! I'm going to break my ankle running on these stupid things. When I think I can't take one more step, Luc pulls up. I'm so thirsty it hurts to swallow.

'What the hell,' gasp, pant, '. . .they would have . . .' I want to say, 'they would have let us walk out' but I'm too busy gasping.

'They thought we were spies.' Luc puffs and pants as well.

Good, so I'm not the only unfit one.

'Took half an hour of sweet-talking at the gate to let me come in. Everyone's paranoid.'

Marianne steps out from behind some timber crates. She leaps up and hugs me. I want to hug her back but I need space to breathe.

Worry is writ large over her face. 'We thought we'd never see you again.'

'No time for that,' Luc says, 'We have to get out of here.'

'Hang on.' This stonewall is so lovely and cold to lean against. 'Need to rest first.' It's getting darker, but the streetlights have not come on. Now that I have a second to look around, I don't see poles with lights on them.

Luc gives us less than a minute to recover. 'We must keep going. If you can't run, at least walk quickly.'

Can't swallow. Need a drink. As I fall in behind Luc and Marianne, I look around for shops so I can buy a bottle of water to gulp down. No shops open. That's weird. This place is usually crawling with tourists. Another thought piggybacks on the last one. 'Where are all the cars?'

Marianne is puffing like she's the one who's been running. 'Luc, stop, we need to tell Ingrid what's happened.'

'There'll be time for that when we're on the train,' Luc says without a backwards glance. I had his full attention back at the nun's place, now he doesn't care about me. So it was just an act for the nuns. Should have realised.

'Where are we going?' A girl needs to know these things.

'Away from here. Away from the front. We'll get to Paris first and then we can work out where to go after that.' Luc sounds like he knows what he's talking about. Except –

'But our family is in Reims!' Marianne says.

'The Germans have it surrounded. Paris is safer,' Luc says. 'We'll be at the station soon.'

They're talking like we're still doing cosplay. Luc's taking the re-enactment way too seriously. One of my Mum's sayings pops out. 'Put a man in uniform and it goes to his head.'

Luc doesn't slow down.

I try the softer target. 'Marianne, have you got your mobile phone? We should call our parents to let them know we're all right.'

Something rumbles in the distance, like thunder but . . . too deep and sub-woofery. The ground shakes into my feet and trembles through my knees. An earthquake? Luc had the right idea about getting out of here as fast as we can.

Marianne gasps and stumbles. I help her up and sweep the dust off her knees. Her eyes fill with tears. She must have fallen hard.

'I don't have my phone," she says. "Try not to get upset, but if you had your phone, it wouldn't work. Look around.'

What have I missed? Normally it's a job and a half filtering everything out so I can focus on what I'm supposed to be doing. Now I've missed something. Looking around again, it hits me. No phone towers. Something wobbles in my guts and it's not from the ground rumbling. I have a horrible feeling we are in serious trouble. Wait a minute. 'Why are all the road signs in English?' We're in France, right?

Luc frowns at me, then looks at the sign. He shrugs and says, 'Reims is spelt the same way in French and English.'

'Yeah but, it's missing those accents and thingies.'

'Paint shortages,' Luc says.

'That's in English. Look, *Great Northern Road*.'

That shuts Mr Know-It-All up. For a second. Until he says, 'Must be to confuse the Germans.'

Oh right. 'But wait, why do we need to confuse the Germans?'

'Stop your squirrel brain and keep moving,' Luc says.

I've gone right off him now.

***

What feels like an hour later, the three of us are panting for breath. I'm beyond thirsty and my feet are killing me. My leg doesn't hurt like it used to, only because the rest of me has surrendered to a universe of pain. We've reached a train station at last. Instead of going to the main ticketing building, Luc leads us around the side of the railway line.

'–' I try to say something.

Luc holds his palm up and shakes his head.

That would be a 'no' then.

He crawls through a hole in the fence and Mari and I follow him, like criminals on the run.

'Why are we –?'

'– no money for tickets,' Marianne answers.

Wait a moment; there aren't any overhead lines here. How do the trains get their power? 'That's a steam train.'

I have a knack for stating the obvious. Soot and dust pepper my eyes and throat. I'm desiccating here.

'You catch on quick,' Luc says as we walk down the side of the line, long past where the platforms end. Why does Luc want to do everything the hard way? The carriages we pass look comfortable enough but we scramble towards a goods van where Luc wrenches the sliding door open.

'Get in.' It's an order. That uniform sure has gone to his head. There is no option but to follow.

In no time at all the train chugs out of the station. All jerks and jumps and rattles. I have no idea where we're going and I can't stop trembling. Maybe from shock, maybe thirst, maybe hunger. Every muscle and joint is burning or aching. My heart is making lurching thumps in my chest.

'Please tell her, Luc. She's falling apart.'

Thanks Mari.

'It's OK.' Marianne gives me a hug but I just want to slump on the ground and die. 'I'm freaking out as well,' she says, 'but we've had longer to get used to it.'

Luc ads, 'We'll get to safety, and then we'll find a way to back to our time.'

'Luc's really smart, he'll work something out,' Marianne says.

That's when my brain snags on something. 'Our time?' If I lie down here for a bit, things will eventually make sense. My stomach contracts and heaves. I'm about to throw up. There's a noise like a barking seal from my throat, but nothing comes out.

'We'll be OK.' Marianne holds my hair back like a best friend. Her voice is like so full of concern I want to cry. What d'you know? I have some moisture left and I'm wasting it on tears.

'The nuns would have thought you were a spy, so we had to get you out of there,' Luc says, apropos of nothing. 'A girl, wearing the French uniform? They would have been insulted beyond words. You were lucky the nuns had you and not some field hospital. The field hospital would have handed you over to the authorities faster than you could sneeze. Nice clothes, by the way.'

I'm trying to control the sharp clenches in my stomach. If I weren't so scared I'd have time to think about how embarrassing this is. Throwing up is not a spectator sport.

Marianne says, 'But I'm still in uniform, you are too. We need to find new clothes like Ingrid.'

Feeling wrung out and clammy-cold, I open my eyes. Why am I still in this nightmare?

There's a rummaging sound and Marianne calls out, 'I found potatoes and carrots.'

'I hate carrots.' The words are out before I can think. Such a dumb thing to call someone. So what if I have orange hair? I didn't choose to have this kind of hair.

In spite of dry heaving, I'm hungry and thirsty. Maybe the carrots will be good for me?

'What is the problem?' Marianne rubs the raw vegetable against her sleeve to clean the skin before biting into it. 'It's good! Here, have one.' She throws me another from the box.

This is definitely a nightmare and I want to wake up. Now please.

'You're allowed to be scared,' Luc says.

I can take anything except the pity on his face. Like I'm Special Needs or something.

Train chugging noises fill the air, every tiny screech of metal pours into my ears. Sensory overload. I definitely haven't had medicine now for how many hours? Can't think straight.

'I'm still amazed by the fact that we're here,' Luc says. 'I haven't worked out how it happened. I think we are the only ones though. I haven't seen anyone else from the re-enactment.'

My stomach rumbles so I take a bite of the carrot. Loud and crunchy, almost juicy like an apple. Except for the dirt finding its way between my teeth. Eating makes almost enough noise to drown everything else out.

Luc clears his throat. 'I'm going to say it out loud because we're all thinking it anyway. Then we can find a way to deal with it. We've gone back in time.'

Borderline hysterical laughter bubbles out of me, along with a loose bit of carrot.

'You don't believe me? What do you think it is then?' He asks.

I shake my head. 'I'm having a seriously bad dream.'

The way Marianne and Luc exchange glances tells me they've already rejected that theory. Probably a few others as well.

'This is real, Ingrid,' Marianne says. 'On the battlefield, it became real. We walked back to you but you vanished, then we fell through time.'

Cold fear ripples through me. 'That's not what happened at all.' In spite of the fact I hate carrots, this one is surprisingly tasty-juicy. 'You guys were walking toward me and you just went, like that,' I click my fingers, except I'm shaking so much it doesn't work. 'It all felt so real and . . . a bit wrong . . . but so real it –' Oh great, now Luc's gone from giving me the pity look to something . . . strange.

'I'm not laughing at you. That's how I felt too.'

Marianne stops chewing for a Moment. 'I think we are here for a reason. History must need us.'

That sounds pretty arrogant, but I keep this thought to myself. I'm also not totally sold on the time travel theory. 'If we're back in time, why did those nuns all speak English?'

'Maybe they're a special order,' Marianne says with a shrug. 'Some nuns take a vow of silence, maybe others take a vow of English?'

Time travel *would* explain the seriously warped telephone though. And having to use a . . . what did they call it? Interpreter? No. Connector? Can't remember. That other woman on the phone who yelled at me. 'OK then, what about the road signs being in English?'

'I already told you. To confuse the Germans who are invading France right this minute,' Luc says. 'Which is why I got us on this train to get us out of danger. Oh please, stop heaping praise on me for saving your lives, it's embarrassing.'

'Ease off the sarcasm,' Mari says.

Thunder rolls in the distance and I peer through a crack in the rattling timber wall to look outside. It's dark and slick with rain.

It was raining when we fell through time.

'Maybe, if we have travelled in time, some kind of cosmic force has sucked us in by mistake. Like a black hole.' I count to three, waiting for Luc and Marianne to laugh. They don't.

'I like your theory,' Luc says.

His compliment unfurls daisy petals of hope. Then the self-hatred kicks in. Why am I so desperate for a compliment from him? I'm pathetic!

'I think we're here because somebody needs us,' Marianne says.

Not a bad theory either. That's all we've got. Theories. If you accept the theory of time travel, which I'm starting to think is possibly the only way any of this makes sense.

The train rocks unevenly as we trundle down the line. May as well search through the boxes for more food.

Mari wipes her forehead. 'Why would you fill a train with empty boxes?'

Luc sounds like he knows what he's talking about. 'They would have been full of guns and ammo when they arrived at the station. They're sending them back to the depot for refilling. It's how we had an advantage over the Germans, we had better supply lines.'

'But, they're just boxes?'

'Everything is in short supply, so everything is reused or recycled. When the train gets to Paris, they'll fill them up again with weapons and food for the trenches and send the train back to where the soldiers are.'

He must have read that somewhere in a book. Nobody just *knows* that stuff.

'And you're sure this train is going to Paris?' Marianne chomps into another carrot.

Luc spreads his hands out. 'Where else would it go?'

'Great!' I need to sit on the floor. Knees tucked under my chin. Any second now I'll start sucking my thumb and rocking. 'It's real, isn't it? It's really happening. We're really here, in the First World War. This is for real!'

Luc nods. 'Heads up, if we talk to anyone, we shouldn't say, 'First World War'. They don't know about the second one yet. We should just say 'the war' because at this point in time, everyone thinks this one is the war to end all wars.'

My head is going to crack open.

'If it makes you feel any better, I thought I was dreaming too, at first,' Marianne says.

'But we know we can't all be in the same dream,' Luc says. 'I'm not dreaming. Are you dreaming, Ingrid?'

'No.' If this were really a dream, you'd be kissing me. Something flips in my belly. Oh Jesus did I say that out loud? Why is he looking at me so funny?

An uncomfortable silence descends as the train chugs on, taking us closer to Paris. The smells of sawdust, grease and our collective perspiration fills the cabin. Time to breathe through my mouth. 'What year did they invent deodorant? I reek.'

Luc moves over towards me and takes my hands in his. If it were just the two of us holding hands, it would be nice, but we are in the eye of the insanity storm. And I stink and I'm scared out of my brain so I can't enjoy it at all.

'We're going to be OK. We know our history. We're the lucky ones. We know how this ends which means we know how to stay out of trouble.'

'How can you be so calm? This is freaking me out.' Because he sounds way too comfortable with the situation.

At least he's not making fun of me.

'Don't stress. I'll take care of you. Both of you,' Luc says, looking from me to Mari and back again.

Didn't realize I needed the reassurance so badly. Didn't notice my shoulders up around my ears. This huge sigh comes out and I sag like a flat tyre. When Luc puts his arms around me, I slump into him. Nothing romantic, not even remotely, yet his strong embrace is exactly what I need.

I'm still wondering if it's all a crazy dream when the train guard walks in and points a gun at us.

– FOUR –

'DESERTERS!' The guard screams.

What rickety teeth he has! Oh yeah, and the gun. He points it at Luc.

'How dare you leave the fighting! Men are dying because you are not there to help them!'

'He's not a soldier!' Marianne cries out, competing with the rollicking noise of the train.

Luc puts his palms up in surrender. 'Calm down Mari, I can tell him myself –'

The guard doesn't want to calm down. His gun-holding hand is trembling with rage. 'Hang your heads in shame! Who is your commanding officer? You will be shot for this!'

'I don't have a commanding officer because I'm not a soldier.' Beads of sweat break out above Luc's top lip. Good luck getting the guard to believe that, especially when they're still wearing the uniforms.

The old scroat isn't pointing the gun at me because I'm stuck in this oldendays costume. The nuns saved my skin. But Luc and Mari are in a heap of trouble.

'Merde!' Marianne takes off her hat and her long hair falls over her shoulders. 'Please. We are not deserting our posts. We are children.'

A look of horror spreads over the guard's craggy face. He swears under his breath and stomps over to the connecting door to the guard's wagon. Without taking his eyes off us, he pulls the brake cord. Alarms and brakes shriek in the air. The world lurches sideways, throwing me to the ground. For a split second, I wonder if this is like that movie *Inception* and the jolt will wake me up.

Nope. Still on the train. The guard is still pointing his gun at Mari.

Wait a minute. Why is the guard speaking English? Mari and Luc are answering him in English as well.

Maybe I've whacked my head and I can understand French? My stomach folds in on itself as crooked teeth man points his gun at me. My hands are up in the air–so are Mari and Luc's–our voices are fighting each other.

'Don't shoot!' Luc says.

'– Not armed.' Mari says

'We surrender.' Call me a coward, but I don't want to die.

'I can explain!' Luc starts.

'It's not what it looks like.' I'm trying to help. Because it must look really bad. A soldier not travelling with his men and a girl in a soldier's uniform. It must be right up there with the all-time greatest insults to crusty old grandpas.

'We're not in the army, we're only sixteen!' Luc says. His voice squeaks in the middle.

Why do I feel even sicker knowing he's just as terrified as me?

Luc keeps explaining, 'We signed up, we looked old enough but they found out the truth about our age and turned us back. We're going to Paris to try again.'

Doubt clouds the old man's face. We're jolted again as

the train comes to a complete stop. For a second I think the guard believes us, because he lowers the gun. But then I notice it's to aim it at Mari's legs, not her chest.

'You're a girl, why are you insulting the uniform?'

'She had a stupid idea to enlist,' Luc says. 'She's always acted like a boy. We're twins, you see, but I came out first and when she came out she was blue. She's a bit . . . wrong in the head. I tried to stop her . . .'

Hang on. He said I was funny upstairs when he got me away from the nuns. Is he going to pretend we're idiots every time we're in trouble?

'Liberty, equality, brotherhood or death.' Marianne recites the national motto of France. Then she adds, 'We fight together or we die.'

The guard lowers the gun. He clicks it in his hand, which I hope means he's put the safety back on. Is there such a thing as a safety switch or is that just some Hollywood myth? Shut up brain. I need you to shut up now.

The guard turns to Luc. 'You don't look sixteen. You look twenty to me.'

'But he is. He's barely started shaving,' Marianne says.

Luc glares holes through her.

Nice one Marianne. I'd give her a high-five if things weren't so tense.

'Get off the train.' The guard yanks the loading door open. 'You're an offense to the uniform.'

Luc says, 'But we're going to Paris to enlist.'

'And I'm having breakfast with Napoleon. Now get off the train!'

Marianne isn't arguing. She's already half way out the door and scrambling down the side of the carriage. Smart girl that Mari. I'm only a heartbeat behind her, using whatever I can find as a foothold. Suddenly there's nothing for my feet to settle on and I'm all stretched out.

Nothing for it but to drop the last metre. Pain shoots up my bad leg and I land on my arse. At least I'm off the train.

The uniform has gone to Luc's head because he acts invincible and jumps the whole way down.

He lands with a grunt. '*Zut*! My ankle!'

'Get up.' Marianne sounds shirty.

'I'm serious.' Luc sucks in a breath. 'It's swelling already.'

We move away from the train in a group hobble. 'Hold still,' I need to get a better look at his injury. If he has one. My eyes adjust to the low light as I lift the hem of his trousers. I can make out the silhouette of his boot and a muffin-top shape above it. I can't see much so I gently run my palms over his skin. I swear, I am not trying to cop a feel, his calf really is swollen. 'Not good.'

'And painful.' Luc leans on me for balance.

'Um, guys, we better get moving.' There's a quaver in Mari's voice. 'Old man's got his gun out again.'

In a mess of arms, legs and grunts, Mari and I clamp Luc's arms over our shoulders and start five-legged-racing across the uneven ground. Four and a half legs if you count my wound as well.

The chug and puff of smoke means the train is moving away, thank goodness. Just as I relax, a gunshot goes off and I leap forward in fright. Totally forgot I had Luc's arm around me, he falls hard over my back. Can't breathe!

Extra pain? No. Which has to mean I haven't been shot. I croak out, 'Are you two OK?'

'Yes,' Mari says. She's all muffled. Must be winded like me.

'Ommpf,' Luc says.

Great gulps wrack me, but I'm breathing again.

The guard yells out, 'Next time I see you, I won't miss!'

'Arsehole,' Mari mutters.

I taught her that.

We're squished down low until we're sure the train is gone. Then it's time to haul back to our feet and check for more damage. So far in my life I haven't broken any bones, and I don't want to start now.

'At least now you have a genuine excuse for not being on the front line,' Mari says to Luc.

'Great. Just great.' Luc's not impressed.

Time to talk about the Elephant in the room. 'So, um, either of you know why he was speaking English instead of French?'

'He was?' Luc looks at me.

I nod.

'I didn't even notice,' Mari says with a crack in her voice.

'Maybe he's an English soldier, posted here for the war,' Luc says.

Nothing is adding up, but in the absence of any other evidence, Luc's idea will have to do. The night is closing in on us. I have to stomp harder to make sure my legs hold firmly enough to take half of Luc's weight. As much as my bad leg might hurt, it's nothing compared to the pain Luc must be in. I'm also trying to mask the fear-shakes. Can Luc feel me trembling?

We pass through a row of trees. The trunks aren't very close together but we have to duck under a few branches, which is physically ridiculous. I'm all elbows and knees.

Once through the trees a farmhouse-shape looms ahead. There are no lights on inside. We hear a snap and flutter of clothing on the line as the wind curls around.

'Let's ask them for help.' I really want to rest and check my leg and Luc's ankle, but I don't want to sound like a sook in front of the others. Would it be cowardly to stop for a while and just hide out?

'Doesn't look like anyone's home,' Marianne says.

Luc grunts with the effort to walk. 'You're forgetting your history, they probably don't have electricity yet.'

My stomach makes another embarrassing, squelching sound. 'Sorry.'

'I'm hungry too,' Marianne says.

We keep stumbling until we reach a woodpile as tall as us. Nearby there's a large stump with an axe jammed in it. It feels so good to stop and breathe for a minute. Luc rests his injured leg on a block of wood to keep it raised.

I lift my skirt to squint at my injury, amazed at how much I can see despite the darkness. My eyes must have grown accustomed. The nuns have done a great job; the bandage is neat and clean.

'What's that?' Luc's voice is full of concern as he puts a hand on my shoulder.

'Oh, nothing, just a bullet wound.' That sounds so cool.

'For real?'

'Yeah, but it's only a scrape.' I unravel the bandage, rolling it up as I go round my leg. 'Is there a tap? I can wash this out and wrap your ankle with it instead. Remember RICE for first aid. Rest, Ice, Compression and Elevation.'

'I think . . .' Marianne squints and points towards the house. 'That looks like the handle of a water pump.'

'Taps haven't been invented yet?'

'Girls, don't worry about it, I'm feeling better now,' Luc says.

'Really?' I don't believe him. Before he can stop us, Mari and I get to the tap and pump at the handle until water sloshes out. Freezing cold. I have no idea if the water is clean, but I'm so thirsty I stick my face under it and guzzle. Mari too. It's like ice jabbing straight into my stomach but it's water and it's beautiful. Don't tell me about whatever dead things might be in the well and we'll all be fine.

Luc winces as he moves his foot. He unlaces his boot

and it takes both Mari and I a few tugs to get it off.

Mari says what I'm thinking, 'How will we get it back on?'

I work quickly and make figure-eights with the icy wet bandage to support the joint. You don't play netball all your life and not know how to strap an ankle.

Despite being the patient, Luc keeps on thinking he's in charge. 'We need to eat, and we need new clothes. If there are people in the house, they might help. But before we knock on the door, we need to get our stories straight because everyone's suspicious of strangers around here.'

I wonder if they'll speak English or French in the house?

Marianne makes a noisy sigh. 'OK, you are a wounded soldier. But so help me, if you say I am stupid again your nose will be on the other side of your face.'

Luc laughs it off. 'I promise.'

I finish strapping Luc's ankle. 'Thank you, it feels better already,' he says, and touches my cheek. Brain jolt. If he doesn't move his hand soon, he'll feel the heat racing up my face.

'It's nothing.' Time to retreat to the shadow of the woodpile.

Marianne is looking up. 'Whoa, look at all those stars!'

Patchy cloud cover obscures some areas, but I've never seen the night sky so sparkly. Sitting still like this gives the evening chill time to sneak in. Funny how I'd been so preoccupied with running away to notice the cold.

'They're so bright.' Luc's words come out in a breath. Probably because his foot still hurts even though he's pretending it's better.

Stargazing with Luc. My insides fizz with romantic possibilities. There is something very wrong with me to be thinking like that. Maybe it's because it's just the three of us, maybe it's the adrenaline rush of nearly dying. Maybe I'm just a mental case with a squirrel brain. It's not like I can do much about it. I try to filter what's important and what's not, but some days it's like even the wind in the trees is screaming at me and my head's so full I can't sort anything out.

'Yeah, wow,' Marianne says.

Luc says, 'Let's rehearse our stories I'm a wounded soldier. My company has been wiped out– *merde*, get down!'

He pushes me face-first into the ground. The hell, man? Luc's holding me down and mouthing 'sorry' to me. Like that makes it OK? He points to a gap in the woodpile and makes me take a look.

Oh *merde* all right. There is a man in uniform, his rifle slung over his shoulder. He's puffing on a cigarette. Mustn't be French then, because otherwise he wouldn't bother to smoke outside.

Between puffs on the cancer stick, he swigs from a flask. Luc's hand rests on my shoulder and he mouths the word 'German'.

Icy terror roots me to the spot. If the German soldier sees us, we're dead.

– FIVE –

STOMACH churning with fear, I press against Luc's body for safety. No, I'm not just trying to cop a feel! Someone on the other side of the woodpile will mow us down if they spot us. Only minutes ago we were going to knock on the door and ask for help. That would have been a seriously stupid plan.

The back door creaks open, then bangs shut. Does that mean the soldier has gone in or has someone else come out? Dammit, there's another man's voice. But we've got our answer. Two enemies by the back door now. Double the danger. A drumbeat pounds in my head. Tremors kick into my legs so hard I have to lock my knees together to hold them tight. Damp night air seeps into my bones. I have to clamp my teeth shut to ward off an attack of the shivers. I am so not cut out for this level of stress.

The chill spreads in strange ways; a patch on my lower back starts to ache, goose bumps spread over my neck. A cramp of cold takes hold near my kidneys. Breathing through my nose is bringing on brain freeze, but if I breathe through my mouth my teeth will start jack-hammering together.

Marianne holds her thumb and finger over her nose and makes a shaky-jerk movement.

And again.

No way, she cannot be sneezing!

Every shudder of Marianne's body sends fresh bursts of fear through me. She is going to sneeze out loud any moment now and give us away. If we stay here, it's suicide. Especially with Luc and Marianne wearing such authentic French army clothes. We had a hard time explaining the uniforms to an old bloke on the train, and he was on our side. How could we possibly explain ourselves to Germans?

Call it a hunch, but they probably won't be speaking English.

We have to get out of here. I tap Luc on the arm and resort to sign language. I point to me, then point to the trees. Luc blinks, then looks up at the sky.

What?

Oh! I get it. The moon is almost behind a cloud. It will be darker soon. Better coverage.

The back door swings open and bangs shut again. Have the soldiers gone in?

A third voice. Jesus Christ, how many Germans are there?

Keeping low to the ground, Luc peers through the gaps in the logs, trying for a glimpse. His shoulders slump. Not a good sign.

'How many?' I mouth when he turns back.

Luc holds up four fingers.

Four!? I'll be dead from a heart attack before they can shoot me. But then a new thought gives me strength. We did not get sucked through time just to get shot. That can't be how this works.

Our enemies are talking amongst themselves, making enough low noise to help us out a bit. As long as we're careful, they won't hear us sneaking off.

The cloud covers the moon. This is our chance.

Luc puts his mouth to my ear and murmurs, 'Stay low. Keep crawling until you get to the tree line and wait for us there.'

A moment ago, I was ready to sprint. Now it's really happening, lead fills my belly and fear immobilises me. I don't want to be the first, but at the same time I don't want to get left behind. I have to go now or we're all dead.

No more thinking, only doing. I'm as low to the ground as I can get. Wet grass tickles my face. My clothes turn wet, then icy, dragging me down. I have to keep moving. Don't think, squirrel brain, just move. You're in a first-person game, everything is made of pixels, you can focus. I should be offended that Luc called me 'squirrel brain', but it's true so I'm going to own it.

Keeping the woodpile directly behind me to provide cover, my best chance is that the moon doesn't come out. I'm shivering all over and clamping my mouth shut, breathing through my nose. Every breath is an act of defiance.

Keep going, keep going.

The safety of the trees is agonizingly far away.

Crawl, crawl, crawl. The stupid long skirt catches my knees. The waistband slips and slows me down. For a second I look back and see a lumpy shape moving towards me. It must be Marianne.

I hope it's Marianne.

Back towards the house I see the glow of cigarettes.

A horrible thought worms into my brain. If I can see them, they can see us.

The trees, the trees, get to the trees.

Every second feels like forever as I shuffle-crawl along.

The tree trunks come closer. I want to run the last few paces but my skirt's fallen down.

'Ht-zzzt!'

Oh *merde*. Marianne just sneezed.

Panic sets in. I jump to my feet then fall over my skirt. Fumbling now, I grab what I can of the skirt and race for the trees, not stopping until I'm safely behind them. My cowardly streak wants to keep running but I have to stop and make sure Marianne's OK.

Dammit, the moon's come out.

Marianne is achingly close, but Luc's nowhere.

Double *merde*, he's still by the woodpile.

'Halt!' One of the soldiers calls out. He's looking over the field, at Marianne.

'Run!' Funny how you can whisper and shout at the same time.

Like a rabbit, Marianne shoots off the ground towards me. The soldier takes aim.

'Zigzag!'

A shot rings out. Marianne stumbles and lurches. Did they hit her?

No. They missed. Marianne recovers and runs to me.

A metallic click carries on the wind. The soldier has re-loaded.

Hot sick burns the back of my throat. Finally, Marianne makes it to the trees and falls over in a heap. I can't ask if she's all right. I can't even move for fear. Luc is still stranded by the wood heap.

Through the moonlight, I see a glint of metal behind the soldier. The silhouette of a man is closing in behind him.

It's Luc. He's got the axe from the chopping block.

More soldiers come out of the house.

Luc swings the axe. The man with the gun topples with a sickening grunt. The German soldiers by the house get their guns ready.

Marianne pants for breath. She sees what's going on and screams.

'Run!' I yell as loud as I can. Oh God he's going to die! In the next breath, I turn to Marianne. Yes, self-preservation is selfish, but if we don't move, we're dead too.

'Get up, Mari, run.'

'What about Luc?'

I can't see him. Oh God, have they got him? Ohthankgod. Luc's taken off in a different direction, racing into the darkness.

The soldiers fire at him.

'They're going to kill him!' Mari takes a step towards the house. I pull her back with all my strength and keep her behind the tree with me.

'He'll be OK, he'll be OK.' I'm lying to myself more than her.

More shots ring out. I cover my ears but tears burst out. Grief, fear, cold, you name it. It's all too much. We're going to die.

How long are we standing here, by the tree, looking at dark shapes through the night, wondering who is who?

In the distance is the sound of feet padding hard on the ground. An uneven step. Another soldier? We're finished.

'Run!' It's Luc, closing in fast.

Joy surges through me. Luc is alive, and he's saved my life. Saved *our* lives. Brainsplosion, I think I'm half in love with his bravery right now.

'RU-UN!' Injured ankle or not, Luc doesn't slow down as he charges past us.

He looks magnificent.

We're not out of danger yet. Gunfire tears through the night with more yelling in German. I'm on my feet, grabbing Marianne with me and charging after Luc. Must be fear and adrenaline pushing him at such a pace. All I know is we're going fast and we can't stop. Fear has me needing to take a wee. Like, seriously, I could just wee as I run and nobody will be any wiser, right? But I'm too busy running to make it happen, so I don't. Probably for the best, right?

My ribs can't expand enough. How long are we running for? Cramp sticks my ribs together. Shouldn't have drunk so much water by the woodpile, it's sloshing inside me. My bad leg feels stiff and sore, but if Luc can run, so can I.

The gunfire stops. We hide behind a pile of earth and dare to look back. Are they following us? Sure we're hiding, but our collective breathing is so loud we may as well be standing in the open. Thump, thump, thump, my pulse hammers away in my neck and head.

'I need to rest or I'll make wafers,' Mari says.

Luc is ignoring her, he's up again and walking. At least he's not running.

No choice but to follow him. Running sure hurt, but walking hurts even more now that I've had a rest. My thighs might as well be made of concrete.

The land angles down and there is splashing ahead. Must be a river. Despite all the water in me, my mouth is dry again and I'm desperate for another drink.

I'll sip it this time.

Luc walks into the water, right up to his knees. A soft groan travels on the wind.

It's not a deep river, but it looks dark and we have no idea what's in it. I'll stay on the shore thanks.

Luc's found a rock the size of a Labrador and is leaning against it. It's hard to tell in the darkness, but I think he's trying not to scream.

The water is so cold it burns my skin. I take a few sips

and although I'm still thirsty, I have to stop or my fingers will snap off.

'Luc, thank you. For everything.' For saving our lives. For making us run when I didn't think we could walk. 'How's your ankle?'

He sucks his breath in over his teeth. Slowly, he makes his way back to the riverbank and sits down, rubbing his good leg to get circulation back into it.

My stomach growls and warbles. 'Sorry.' My head feels too heavy for my shoulders. My hands tremble. Is this fear or exhaustion?

'We need food,' Marianne says.

'One miracle per hour, that's your limit,' Luc says.

A giggle breaks out between us. We are so screwed, yet we're laughing? Here I am in the middle of nowhere–the middle of no-when–and we're laughing.

In the distance is the familiar puffing and rattling of an approaching train. Luc stands up and I follow his lead. Mari gets to her feet as well.

'We should get on that train,' he says. 'Get to Paris, be safe.'

Marianne grabs his arm and pulls him back. 'You're going to jump on a moving train with that foot of yours? Because you were so good jumping off a stationary one.'

'Come on.' He grunts as he walks towards the train line.

It's obvious he doesn't stand a chance. Neither do I for that matter. This long skirt would get caught in the wheels or the gears or whatever those things are. Perhaps the bravery of the last encounter has gone to Luc's head and he feels immortal? Teenage boys eh? They take risks even when they don't need to. He doesn't need to impress me.

'I vote we walk to the nearest town,' Marianne gives me

a tap on the shoulder and I feel lightheaded with relief. It's an excellent suggestion. And safer.

'Good idea Mari.' Doing my best to be supportive. 'I mean, we don't even know where that train is going.'

Luc's words come out staccato as he limps ahead. 'All trains . . . from here go to Paris. So they can . . . bring reinforcements to the . . . front line.'

Stepping in front of him to block his way, Marianne says, 'And where is the front line? Can you tell me that? Can you even tell us what year this is? We don't know anything! All we know is we're some time in the war, but is it the start or the finish? Are we even in France?'

'Don't be stupid. I know my wars, OK. I know my history. If we were in enemy territory, we wouldn't have been let off that other train alive.'

So who were the Germans in the farmhouse then?

'Fine, I'll give you that,' Mari points to the water, 'But if you're so smart, tell me what river this is?'

The train gets closer. Fear holds my tongue down as Marianne and Luc argue about whether we are standing on French soil or not, their voices growing louder by the minute. It turns into shouting as the train and its carriages rattle past.

I put the pieces together too late, but I am totally on Mari's side with this anyway. She's distracted Luc enough for us to miss the train.

'Bravo! Now what?' Luc kicks the ground with his bad leg and grunts.

'I know your leg hurts, and you don't want to let Ingrid see you're in pain,' Marianne says. 'But we need to get to a town, get some help and get some food.'

Heat races up my neck. Does Luc know I'm rocking a crush on him? Maybe it wouldn't be so bad if he knew. If

Luc likes me back, it wouldn't be such a bad thing.

Would it?

Maybe I've moved from Velcro-bonding to hero worship?

'I like Mari's plan,' because I really do. 'Walking might take a while, but we'll find a town soon and surely someone will give us food?'

The earth rumbles. An explosion bursts the sky apart. Mari and I scream and hit the ground so hard I swear I've cracked a rib.

Smoke, flames and burning things fly into the air. So bright I clamp my eyes shut. Chunks of wood and earth and bodies fall to the ground.

The enemy has blown up the railway line, taking out the train Luc wanted us to get on.

Fear, revulsion and relief flood through me. If we hadn't killed ourselves climbing on the train in the first place, we would have been blown to bits.

By having an argument, Marianne has saved our lives.

– SIX –

I CAN'T take my eyes off the smouldering ruin that was the train.

'That was . . .' Luc gulps. 'We nearly . . .'

Yeah. We so nearly did.

Marianne grabs her brother and hugs him hard. Then she grabs me and squishes us in a three-way relief-clench.

The wind carries moans and cries from the injured. Then somebody barks orders in German. Not French, not even English. Have we accidentally wandered into the wrong country?

Marianne jolts us out of the hug. 'We have to get away, agreed?'

Good plan! I'm nodding so much my head's gonna snap off. How long until the area is swarming with men wearing exactly the wrong kind of uniform? Luc and Marianne are still wearing their French army clothes, and something tells me that the other lot don't care for our sort.

At least Mari has her head on straight, because mine's turned to custard. 'We follow the tracks away from here,' she says, 'back to the nearest town. Yes? We need food, and we need to get out of these damn clothes. Otherwise we are walking targets.'

The cold water and adrenaline must be wearing off. Luc staggers forward, his shoulders slumped. Mari and I take an arm each side to support his weight. The rank tang of BO has me mouth-breathing. Again.

I have this mega-strong sense of smell. Mum calls it a blessing and a curse. I can smell gas leaks when I walk past houses on the way to school. I was late one day because I stopped and knocked on the door to tell them I could smell gas. That spoiled egg kind of smell. It made me late for school more than once, so I ended up making little notes that I could put in people's mailboxes instead.

We've staggered further from the train wreck when fear brings me back to earth. 'How do we know there aren't more Germans between here and the town?'

Luc grunts as he hobbles between us. 'If they were closer to town, they would have blown the train up earlier, don't you think?'

'OK.' It kind of makes sense. 'But what if they're advancing on the town now?'

'Then we'd better get there before they do,' he says.

Through the night we walk alongside the train tracks, occasionally stumbling but moving ever onwards.

'What town are we going to again?' I squint, wondering if the dark shapes to the side of us are houses or my imagination playing tricks. A signpost comes into view.

Amiens.

'I don't . . . I'm not sure why, but the name sounds familiar. 'Luc, you know your history, why is Amiens important?'

'There was a battle near here, but I'm not exactly sure when it was.'

Marianne stops. 'You're not sure? But you know everything about the war!'

What the hell? Mister History has a glitch?

'Do I look like Wikipedia? I know some stuff, but not a blow-by-blow account, OK?'

A man, possibly in his late fifties judging by his stubbly white whiskers and worn face, is up ahead. 'Guys, stop arguing, we've got company.' He's got a curly moustache like those men in the trenches. The ones that, I realise now, must have been real soldiers, not part of our dress-ups. I hope this bloke isn't judgmental like the old man on the train.

Luc limps towards him. 'The enemy has blown up the railway line, taking out the last train that left here, in that direction.' He points behind him. 'We jumped clear and came as soon as we could. The line to Paris is not safe. Get a message to the generals right away.'

So confident, so fast. Luc is full of surprises.

The old man salutes and runs back to the station building.

'What do you know? The uniform came in handy.' Luc grins.

Looking along the platform, I see a small shack. 'Is that a toilet up ahead? I'm busting.'

Just then, the wind carries the stink toward us.

Marianne's nose crinkles as she smells it too.

'On second thoughts, maybe not.' Gah, it's worse than the back of Flinders St Station. What is it with train stations and people taking a slash wherever they like?

Luc points. 'There are some bushes over there.'

'That's OK for you, you're not a girl.' Marianne looks around for somewhere more decent to go. Maybe we can find a take away in town where we can have a Mc Piss? Have they invented Hungry Jacks yet?

From the looks of it, nobody has any lights on. Does anybody have electricity? Oh, hang on, there's a war on. Maybe they're keeping their lights off so the bombers can't find them. Do they have bombers in this war? I have no idea.

We hobble towards the terminal building, Luc stumbles and lurches between us. If we're lucky, the local doctor might take us in. Especially with an injured soldier in tow.

'We smell worse than a dead cat on a hot day,' Marianne says.

All that running and stress makes me acutely aware of the stink I've worked up. The nuns gave me clothes, but not deodorant. The running must have shaken the nit-powder from my hair, because I can't smell that any more. Just body stench and fear. 'I wonder when hot showers were invented?'

'Maybe we could invent them,' Luc says, his breath coming out in gasps every time he puts weight on his bad ankle. 'Right after we invent bubble wrap, mobile phones and MP3 players.'

'Har-har. I'm sure that is exactly why we are here,' Marianne says.

Something rankles with me. 'Should we have told the station master about the Germans blowing up the train?'

'Of course!' Luc says.

Because I've seen far too many time travel shows and I know the rules. 'What if by telling him what's happened, we've somehow altered things. And we don't know if we've altered them the right way?'

'The stationmaster would have found out anyway, it's not like we've interfered . . . much,' Luc says.

'Ingrid has a point,' Marianne comes to my defence. 'We have to be careful what we say to people. An innocent comment might be interpreted the wrong way. Or it might have some kind of domino effect and change history. We don't want the Germans to win, do we?'

'And you are an expert on time travel all of a sudden?' Luc sounds tetchy.

'Are you saying we shouldn't be careful?' Marianne sounds

just as tetchy.

Times like these I'm grateful for being an only child. 'Please don't fight. The station master's coming back.'

Luc and Marianne clamp their mouths as the old man approaches.

'You are injured. Come with me,' he says. 'My wife will find you rooms. Our sons are in the army. Perhaps you have met them? Which division are you in?'

Dread climbs up my throat. The man's very own flesh and blood are giving their lives for the cause while we're playing dress-ups.

'Then they are true men of France and I wish I was with them,' Luc says. There is a confidence in his voice I haven't heard before. Borderline patronising, but I guess he's doing his best to sound like a battle-weary soldier from olden times instead of a pretender from two thousand and sixteen.

'We volunteered to join the sixth army, but they found out how young we were. They sent us home.' Luc is so convincing I half believe it.

'Our mother,' Marianne says. 'She demanded they release us.'

The station master stops and stares at Marianne. 'You're a girl!

At which point, hello, he's speaking fluent English and I just don't think things are making any sense at all. Aren't these people proud Frenchies? What are they doing speaking the language they're supposed to hate?

Mari stands tall. 'I love my country as much as any man!'

'Ha!' He slaps her hard on the shoulder. 'A regular *Maid of Orléans*!' Then he looks me up and down. 'What is your story? Did you try to enlist as well?'

'I'm their cousin.' The lie is out before my brain knows what my mouth is up to.

'From Australia,' Mari adds.

'Then you are a long way from home,' he says.

You don't know the half of it.

'I am Georges Gaillard.' He shakes all our hands and we do a quick bit of introducing ourselves before he leads the way towards a stone building nearby. 'My wife will take delight in mothering you to death. She misses her boys. They are in the fifth army. If she asks, tell her Robert and Pierre Gaillard are safe and well.'

When we reach the house, Luc embraces Georges. 'God be with you.'

Why haven't Luc and Marianne noticed we're all speaking English. Anyone, anyone?

Georges' wife opens the door, looks at us with sleepy eyes. 'Robert? Pierre? Is that you?'

'Put your spectacles on woman.' Georges doesn't protect his wife's feelings as he turns to Luc. 'She sees our sons' faces in all people. This is my charming wife Mathilde, she will find a bed for you for the night.'

Mathilde speaks English like a natural as well. There's a slight French accent to her, a bit like the way some Canadians who speak French have a bit of the 'eh' in them. What are they called? Oh yeah, French Canadians. Because last year we had a student at school, Anny, who was not Canadian, she was *French Canadian*. Oh please, brain, stop thinking every darn thing and just let me get some peace and quiet for a while. I'm so dog-tired but I bet I lie awake tonight, mind racing getting zero sleep.

Speaking of no sleep, how cavalier of Georges to wake his wife from her bed and tell her to take people in.

Instead of cracking the sads, Mathilde embraces us and brings us inside. The kitchen is marinated in years of cooking smells. Melted cheese. Stewed meat and vegetables. Fried onions. The rooms are poky with low ceilings. And there aren't that many of them either. How are we all going to fit?

A softening fire crackles in the hearth. Mathilde adds more wood to it, then brushes the splinters and dust from her hands and smoothes them down the front of her dressing gown.

'What did he mean by *Maid of Orléans*?' I whisper to Marianne.

'Joan of Arc. A warrior like no other.'

'Didn't she get burned to death or something?'

'Only after she led a vast army to victory against the English.'

Time to mention what's been bugging the hell out of me. 'You've noticed they speak English, haven't you?' Either that or at some point I've whacked my head and I can understand French all of a sudden. Yeah, but no.

'Please sit.' Mathilde indicates the nearby wooden table and chairs, the kind that look like they've taken a beating over the decades.

'I think she is speaking English,' Marianne says beneath her breath. 'As am I. It doesn't make sense.'

'Good, so I'm not going mad.' I don't think Luc has even noticed yet. Maybe his ankle is hurting so much he can't focus on anything other than the pain. Maybe that's what I should do; break my foot so the only thing I can do is hurt, instead of this constant thinking, thinking, thinking.

By the fire, Mathilde swings the iron support arm out to stir the heavy pot hanging from it. It's a classic witch's cauldron. Savoury smells waft around the room as she stirs the soup with a long handled spoon.

Luc makes himself comfortable in a wooden chair, resting his bad leg on a stool beside him. He's too far away for us to quietly mention how everyone is speaking the same language and it isn't French.

I'm trying to behave, but I need to use the facilities right now.

'Is the bathroom down the hall?'

'Heavens no, why would you think that?' Mathilde bangs her spoon on the side of the pot, then walks over to the kitchen door and lets in the cold night air. 'It is at the end of the path.'

An outdoor toilet? I'd rather die. On the other hand, I really, *really* need to go.

The tiny outhouse looms ominous and revolting. Something scurries in the darkness. I don't want to know what it is. What the heck, it's dark, nobody will see. I find a patch of grass and use that instead.

Back inside, Mari takes her turn while I wash my hands in the kitchen sink, then sit down to an enormous bowl of soup and some crusty bread. My stomach growls and grumbles, the soup burns my tongue on the way down. Luc is dipping his bread into the soup and I follow his lead.

Such a simple meal, but it's perfect.

Mari joins us inside and I can tell by her face that she found the toilet and didn't like it. But what else can we do? The insanity of the day catches up with me and I'm practically falling asleep in the chair. The noises in my head soften to a dull roar. That's when I look over and see Mathilde creating make-shift beds for us on the flagstone floor.

We are in for a rough night.

– SEVEN –

THE next morning, I wake stiff and sore, like I've slept on stones. Oh, that's right, I have. Flat stones on the ground, no mercy for muscles. Joints cramp as I twist and stretch them back to life. In the garden, a rooster crows to raise the sun.

Has it only been a day since we travelled? So much has happened I can barely get my head around it.

'Time to make breakfast girls.' Mathilde fusses with the fire to keep it burning. She's wearing a drab, off-white dress with a dirt-stained pinafore over the top. Marianne coughs from the smoke as she dresses in a similar outfit. High collar, lots of buttons down the front, long skirt over her army boots.

A quick look under the blanket reminds me I've slept in my clothes. God I reek! 'What time is it?' Breath steams in front of my face. Even with the fire starting up, it's close to freezing in here.

Nearby on the floor–closer to the fire, Luc sleeps on. His freshly bandaged foot is elevated on a pile of old clothes.

'Wake up Luc, time for breakfast.'

Mathilde rushes over. 'No, no, no. He is injured, he must rest.'

The corners of Luc's mouth tilt up in a smile.

Faker!

The morning trip to the outside toilet is worse than the night before. In the early light I can see the filth instead of just imagining it. Mould and cobwebs everywhere. Can you really catch something from sitting on a toilet? I hold myself a couple inches above the seat just in case. Instead of toilet paper, I find newspaper strips jammed onto a rusty nail. I'm trying very hard not to think about how gross everything is as I tear off a page. That's when I see the date along the top of the paper.

January 1916.

Dizziness kicks in. Fear overrides my revulsion at using such basic facilities. We've gone back one hundred years. I get up and turn my face to the bowl. It's not so much a bowl as a long drop into who-knows-what. Heaves cramp my stomach, clamping and clenching but nothing comes out. All I've done is earned a closer look at the old-timey toilet contents and that's not what I need so early in the morning.

The newspaper scraps give me an idea. I rummage through, looking for more dates. The seasons are the opposite of Melbourne, so January means winter. But if it is that early in the year, surely there would be snow all over the place It's cold, but it's not *that* cold. Hunting through the papers, the most recent date I can find is March nineteen sixteen. Which would have to be early spring. I think.

By the time I head back to the house, Marianne is walking out with a basket. 'I've been sent to collect eggs. Care to help?'

Eggs for breakfast sounds brilliant, I link arms with hers and walk lock-step towards the hen house. 'I found out what year it is. We're in nineteen sixteen, some time after March.'

'How did you find out?'

'Um, the er, toilet paper is old newspapers.'

'I thought it felt harsh,' Mari says.

'Ew gross! You didn't use it?'

'I didn't have much choice.' She opens the latch on the chicken enclosure. 'Well done anyway. If you're right, it means we're nearly half way, but the war has another two years to go.'

'And bleach won't be invented for decades.'

Marianne shoots me a strange look, but when she looks back at the dunny block, as we'd call it back in Melbourne, she understands. 'It's not their fault. *Eau de Javel* must be in short supply.'

'So is toilet paper.' My laugh becomes a cough as straw and feathers fly in the air. It's a damp sewer in here. Acrid chicken poop mixed with stale bread and mouldy food scraps make my eyes water. 'Let's grab the eggs and go.' I push my hands under a fat hen's stomach. It's warm and soft, like a fluffy blanket. It's almost enjoyable until the hen pecks my hand. 'Ouch! She bit me!'

'Are you all right? Give me a look.' Marianne examines my hand. A slight scratch, but no broken skin.

'Have you ever collected eggs before?' I try another hen, hopefully this one's not so bitey.

'Our parents took us on a farm holiday years ago,' Mari half squints her eyes as she slides her hand under a chicken. 'They said it would do us good to see where all our food came from. I already knew milk came from cows. They made us get the eggs for breakfast each morning.'

'My folks did that to me too! They took me to a farm so I'd know what I was eating.' I give up trying to steal from this bossy fat hen clucking viciously at me and move on to another nesting box. Third time lucky. Plunging my hands under the warm feathers is kind of nice. This hen gives token resistance and I grab a warm egg.

'Why do parents do that?' Marianne is wistful. 'I was happy to eat lamb and pork and chicken. I didn't need to know it had a face.'

'It's their default position. They like to mess with our heads.' Instead of laughing, a racking sob catches in my throat. Hot tears make everything wobbly. 'Oh God, I miss my Mum!'

'I miss my mother too!'

We forget about the eggs and hold each other, sobbing away.

Mathilde finds us, makes harrumphing noises, and grabs the basket with hardly any eggs in it. 'When you've finished watering the ground, come inside and help cook.' She gathers the rest of the eggs, ignoring the clucking and pecking hens. 'That brother of yours needs a good breakfast if he's to get his strength back.'

Once Mathilde is inside, I turn to Mari. 'You realise she's speaking completely in English, right?'

'Yes, I noticed that. I have no idea why. Do you remember when you asked me ages ago, about how I translate for you, and whether I am thinking in French or English?'

'Yeah?' Because she could translate so quickly, it was as if she was not only speaking in two languages but thinking in them as well.

'That's the problem,' Mari shrugs. 'I don't feel like I'm translating at all, but I must be because I'm talking to everyone in English. Maybe time travel has scrambled our brains?'

'Mine's scrambled for sure.'

Back inside the house, Mathilde leads us to the main bedroom where there's a washstand and mirror. It isn't the shower I'd hoped for, but bless Mathilde, she's filled the bowl with hot water and placed folded towels at the ready. A jar of clear liquid sits beside a fresh sponge. It smells like vinegar.

I scrub my hands and face pink but there isn't much I can do about the hair. Oh look, here's a scarf to tie it off my face and keep my ears warm too.

Only then do I notice my reflection in the mirror.

It makes me scream.

Everything is wrong. My face is round the wrong way. I touch the knot on the scarf and move it to the left. The image in the mirror should mirror me–it's why they're called mirrors, right?

But the Ingrid in the mirror has her scarf knotted on the opposite side like I'm looking into a photograph.

It's all wrong. Wrong, wrong, wrong.

– EIGHT –

'**MARIANNE! MARIANNE!**'

She rushes in. 'What's wrong?'

'This!' With shaking hands I show her the mirror and move my arm left to right. The image shows the opposite. 'It's doing my head in.'

'This is really, really bad,' Marianne says with a gulp. She's standing by my right shoulder, but in the mirror she's flipped.

'What the hell does it mean?' I move my hands, watching them turn the wrong way.

'I . . .' Marianne's face looses twenty percent of her colour. 'I don't know.'

'Girls! What are you doing?' Mathilde bustles in.

My mouth opens and closes, but nothing comes out.

'Well?' Mathilde looks annoyed.

What are we supposed to say?

Marianne clears her throat. 'She's got her period.'

Oh great save there!

'Pardon?'

'Her monthly. You know, The Visitor?'

Mathilde's brows furrow, then realization dawns. 'Ah, the English are here.'

I can't help laughing. I've never heard anyone call it that before. But hang on, she speaks English, so why would that be some kind of . . . oh forget it. Nothing makes sense any more.

Mathilde composes herself and presses her palms down the front of her pinafore. 'I will get you some rags.' Then she adds with a weak smile. 'You are a woman now.'

As soon as she's gone, I smack Marianne on the shoulder. 'Thanks a lot!'

'What else could I say? 'Hi, we're from the future and your mirrors don't work properly. And by the way you should be speaking French?' That would not go down well.'

I rub my forehead, but it's rubbing the wrong way in the mirror and it freaks me out all over again.

'We have to tell Luc,' Marianne says.

'Ew, no we don't.' Then I get it, Marianne wants to tell him about the mirror, not the excuse we gave Mathilde about why I freaked out. 'Oh, yeah, we do.' He might panic, just like us. Then another thought wriggles in. 'Hey, um, when Mathilde said she'd get rags, she didn't mean actual rags did she?'

She did.

Mathilde returns and presses a wad of off-white cloths into my hands. It doesn't matter that I don't really need them. I'm grossed out thinking about the days ahead, when I might need to use them. Unless we can get back to our own time before then. Yes, yes, yes, that sounds like a pretty excellent plan to me.

'I'm not very good at mothering girls,' Mathilde says, pressing her palms to her pinafore again. 'God saw fit to keep my baby girls by his side. But he let me keep my boys and for that I am grateful.' Her chin does a strange wobble and she makes a rapid exit.

Tears come from nowhere and my throat closes up. My words come out as a croak. 'I want to go home.'

Marianne hugs me. The mirror is doing my head in so I slump down to the dusty floor.

'Maybe we're the girls she should have had,' Marianne says.

I can only stare blankly.

'Think about it,' Marianne says. 'God takes her girls, then we turn up. Maybe this is why we came through time. For Mathilde.'

'That's mental.'

'God works in mysterious ways.'

I'm rubbing my forehead. 'Plenty of people lost their babies in the olden days. And . . . and if her girls died when they were babies, like Mathilde said, then she's been waiting a long time for us to show up. Which means God takes his sweet time about things.'

'Oh really?' Marianne's top lip curls.

I know that expression, it's contempt.

How do I explain where I'm coming from? Start with a deep breath, begin at the beginning. 'I know a fair bit about babies and bad chromosomes. And how even if a baby made it, they could die from bad genes or germs.'

'I had no idea you were so scientifically trained,' Marianne says, laying the sarcasm on thick.

'I'm not.' Another deep breath. 'My parents did five rounds of IVF to get me. Mum let me read her diaries when I was twelve, when she thought I was old enough to handle it. It still blows my mind sometimes that I'm even here. But it's all down to scientists helping my parents, not God popping in and answering their prayers.'

It's not fair to dump this on Marianne, but I can't help the resentment bubbling up. Reading Mum's diaries . . . I still don't know if I ever should have. They were so full of anger and hate. But it also explained why they hardly ever went to church.

'Plenty of people told Mum it was God's will whether she had a child or not. But really, it was bad genetics. We know babies don't make it unless every little chromosome lines up exactly right and multiplies and divides just the right way. Poor Mathilde. She's gone through so much, lost her girls when it could be for some kind of genetic reason or maybe some nasty disease we can just get a jab for now, and all she has for comfort are some well-meaning friend saying it's 'God's will', because that's all they know at this point in time.'

Hot splashes fall down my face. Marianne wipes at them with one of the rags.

'Please, not that!'

'Sorry,' Marianne says.

I don't know why I am in such a confessional mode, but the truth keeps coming out. 'My parents never wanted me to be an exchange student. They were terrified something would happen to me. It's hard on them, they can't help being over-protective. And I made them let me come here. I promised I'd stay out of trouble and instead I've nearly been shot twice and we're stuck here and I just want to go home.'

Marianne hugs me. 'We will get home. As soon as Luc's foot is better, we'll find a way to get home.'

'I mean, are they even looking for us now? What if we've been missing for months and we've only been gone a day? Or what if we're gone for months and then get back a minute later? I mean, how does any of it work?'

Did I say that out loud?

'I don't know how time travel works,' Marianne says. 'But I do know that the moment people know we are missing, then all our parents will stop at nothing to find us.'

'That's the thing though. Will they even know we're

missing.'

'Come on, let's eat, I'm starving,' Marianne pulls me up and we walk back to Mathilde.

But instead of a plate of food, Mathilde gives us baskets. 'Ready?' We need to get bread and milk.'

Puzzled, I look around the kitchen and notice there is no refrigerator. Nowhere to keep food fresh.

'Sorry, still a bit tired. We've been overdoing it.' Marianne explains as we step outside.

'I don't believe you girls are telling me the truth.' Mathilde opens the garden gate for us. My stomach sinks to the ground. How does she know?

'You are wealthy, no? You've run away from home or you're running away from a bad marriage?'

Relief washes me clean. She thinks we're rich? That I can deal with. Hang on, what's with the rest of it?
Mathilde gives us an assessing look. 'I believe Ingrid, that you and Luc have eloped and you don't want your parents to find out?'

'Eloped?' Whoa, talk about give a girl ideas.

Mathilde tisks as she leads us down the street towards the town. 'You are keeping secrets. You come from a house with an inside bathroom as you call it, so you must be wealthy. Plus, you all speak The Regent's English, so you are from the upper classes.'

'You speak English as well,' I jump in.

'My mother was a tutor; she wanted me to have opportunities. Whenever we meet strangers, Georges and I speak English first, to see how the other will respond. Let us not change the subject. Despite walking for a day or so, as you told us, I believe none of you have ever done much exercise of that kind before. You're both so fat and tall, from a life of plenty, yet you say you are only sixteen.'

'I'm not fat!' How rude!

'*Pardon*! You are well-fed then. But neither of you have collected eggs or done much in the way of domestic work, which means you must have maids.'

Marianne looks as guilty as I feel. Mathilde's version of the truth is believable, given the circumstances. The real truth will only end in chaos.

'Please, Mathilde, we need some time to adjust,' Marianne says.

Do we ever!

We walk past closed shop fronts. Windows plastered with newspapers. At the bakery it smells delicious despite the depleted shelves. A harried-looking woman comes out from the back kitchen when Mathilde rings the bell.

'Two loaves today, Camille, I have war orphans staying with me.'

We are war orphans? But my parents aren't dead, they just haven't been born yet. Whoa, how crazy does that sound?

The price Camille asks for the bread sounds cheap to me, because I'm thinking in modern day prices, but Mathilde reels in horror at how much she had to pay.

Camille shrugs and says in a heavy accent, 'Everything is expensive. It is getting hard to source good flour.'

It might be accented, but Camille speaks English as well. Seriously, I thought the French hated the English, hated having to speak it, yet here they are, doing it voluntarily.

With a dramatic sigh, Mathilde pays her, takes the loaves and we're back in the cool morning air.

At the dairy, the prices are equally steep. 'These are the same cows you had yesterday!' Mathilde argues.

The farmer shakes his head. 'The army needs half my milk for the soldiers. I cannot refuse, yet I still have a family to feed.'

Guilt stabs me. Mathilde has taken us in, now she's paying for it. I wish we really were rich runaways because then we might have some money to give her. Instead, we're a burden.

On the way home, small groups of people walk quickly between the shops that are still open. They're not stopping to talk much, just a quick greeting as they pass each other and then it's into the next store.

'I know she wasn't trying to be mean when she said we were fat,' Marianne whispers. 'But have you noticed how thin everyone is?'

The blinkers lift from my eyes. Not a chunky to be seen. 'I guess donuts haven't been invented yet.'

Back at the Gaillard's home, Luc is sitting at the table with an end piece of bread and a bowl of steaming soup that must be remnants from the cauldron. Georges is slurping away at his bowl.

'You've decided to join us?' Luc says with a cheeky smile.

Mathilde pretends to scold him but her voice is light and playful. 'Leave the girls alone. They are doing their best.' She heads over to the fire, swings the soup pot out on its arm and drops five eggs, still in their shells, into the soup. And there I was thinking we'd have them scrambled.

I take a seat at the table and pick up the spoon. I can't help looking at my reflection on both sides. I'm sure I should be upside down on one side, but both sides of the spoon give a genuine reflection. Like the way a mirror should work, not like the one from the bedroom.

'Inge, are you still fussing about your hair?' Luc's eyes lock with mine. He gives me a full-beamed smile, which only serves to make my insides squish. Why is he being nice to me all of a sudden?

'The scarf really suits you,' he adds.

That's it, I'm officially confused.

'Dear brother, you need to take a good look at yourself,' Marianne says.

That Mari is a smart one, she knows what she's doing

and I catch on quickly. 'Yes.' I hold the spoon up. 'I highly recommend it. Take a good look at yourself.'

Luc rolls his eyes. 'Girls eh?' He says to nobody in particular.

Georges chuckles.

A strange sense of calm comes over me. The family setting, the friendly banter. It feels so normal and relaxed as we eat the soup Mathilde brings to us. The boiled eggs sit in a bowl, complete with cooked spinach stuck to the shells. Barely a few miles away, people are being blown to pieces. And here we are enjoying a hot breakfast.

Across the table, Luc becomes serious. 'I'm sorry to ask a stupid question, but we've been travelling for a while and have lost track of days. What day is it?'

'Thursday,' Mathilde says.

'Thursday the what?'

'Thursday, April the sixth,' Georges wipes his face with a serviette. 'You've missed being an April Fish.'

'Don't you mean April Fools?' I ask.

Georges screws up his face, then chuckles. 'Is that what you call it in America? You get everything wrong.'

'*Je suis Australien*,' I correct him.

'Interesting, she does speak the common tongue after all,' Georges says.

'So it's April sixth,' Luc repeats, in English for my benefit.

Fear claws at me. He's angling to ask what year we're in, and Mari and I haven't had the chance to tell him we already know the answer to that one. I try to make eye contact with Luc, to give him the message to be quiet. It would be easy enough to get confused about a few missing days here and there, especially without radio and computers. But when someone doesn't know what year they're in, people start thinking about huggy jackets.

A miracle! He looks my way. I make the slightest headshake, hoping nobody else sees.

Georges notices. 'What are you two playing at?'

'Nothing.' *Please shut up Luc.*

A couple of times since our fall through time, Luc has pretended Mari and I are idiots—all in the name of getting out of a scrape. Time to give Luc some of his own medicine. 'He gets confused about dates. He keeps pretending it's only nineteen-ten. Reverting to childhood helps him forget there's a war on.' Will they buy it?

'Yet he wears the uniform?' Georges argues.

That would be a 'no' then.

Marianne places her hand on my arm. 'War does strange things to us all. Something tells me when we look back many years from now, nineteen sixteen will not be seen as a good year.'

Nice save Marianne!

Georges wipes his chin and pushes his chair back. 'Four years of war has turned our brains to mush.' He gives Luc a pat on the shoulder, his wife a peck on the cheek then he heads for the door. 'See you for lunch.'

Four years of war? Hang on. I'm sure Luc mentioned at some point that it started in nineteen fourteen, not nineteen twelve.

Nothing is making any sense.

God? If you can hear me, I've learned whatever lesson it is you want me to learn and I want to go home. Now please.

– NINE –

MATHILDE helps Luc takes a few steps around the room, encouraging him to put more weight on his bad foot. Judging by Luc's cocky smile, he's loving the pampering while Mari and I do all the work. Doesn't matter what century it is, women still do all the unpaid work. Did I just open my mouth and have my mother come out?

No, I was only thinking it, I didn't say it. Thank you brain.

Luc sighs, as if he's the one who's doing all the work.

I'm sweeping the floor. Mari is out in the garden, washing bowls in cold water.

'You cannot be tired,' I say, sweeping the dust into the fire where it crackles and sparks.

'But I am,' Luc says as he takes a seat. Mathilde raises his foot on a nearby stool. Putting a cushion under it too. Sheesh!

'Let him rest,' Mathilde says.

Enabling much?

As soon as Mathilde is gone, Luc picks up a book and sighs again. It's *The Three Musketeers* and for all I know it could be a first edition. Could be worth a fortune.

'I'll wait and see the movie,' he says, tossing it to the floor.

'My heart bleeds,' I give his injured foot a nudge and watch his face. 'Ha! You're fine. Get up and start carrying your weight.'

His face displays shock then anger, 'That's because you kicked the wrong foot!'

'Really? I think I'd remember which one I bandaged.' Heat races up my neck. I was not trying to feel up his leg. I wasn't! 'Get on your feet and start chopping firewood.'

'Be kind to him,' Mathilde says as she comes back to the room. 'He is still recovering.'

'I'm doing my best,' Luc says with a grunt as he stands up. Mathilde fusses about him but he does the whole 'I can do it myself' routine and heads for the door.

In a few moments, the sound of grunting and thwacking fills the air.

'Knowing his luck, he'll chop his foot off,' Marianne says as she returns with clean bowls and plates. Well, clean for a cold wash at any rate.

Mathilde gives a shake of her head and goes outside to help Luc.

I keep my voice low talking with Mari. 'Thank you for letting him know what year it was without making us look like idiots.'

'Yeah, I did OK there, didn't I?'

'Saved our skins. By the way, when Georges made that comment about the war going for four years . . . that wasn't right, was it?'

Mari shakes her head. 'He has to be confused. The war definitely started in nineteen fourteen. We're only two years in.'

Luc hobbles in with three small pieces of firewood. Mathilde follows, carrying about ten. She gives us strange looks and makes tisking sounds as she piles the timber beside the fireplace, then she shakes the splinters off her apron into the fire.

***

We work hard around the house until Georges returns from the railways station for his lunch. It's bread with soft cheese and a bowl of onion and cabbage soup, or whatever vegetables Mathilde has added to that big pot over the fire.

It's a far more relaxed meal than the rush of breakfast, and we even get some entertainment. Nothing as good as Netflix–because it hasn't been invented yet–but the latest in century-old stuff. Mathilde cranks up the back of an enormous box radio and a crackling voice comes out the single speaker on the front.

Georges settles himself into a wing-back chair and puffs on a pipe. The smoke doesn't bother me because the open fire must have already coated my lungs in soot. Plus, it's hiding the heady smells of B.O. and farts. No joke, onion and cabbage soup is nobody's friend.

I'm all set to join the relaxing mood, until Mathilde brings Mari and I a basket of socks, some large needles with wide holes in the end and small balls of yarn. Uh-oh, I failed needlework at school. It was one of those things that required fine motor skills and attention to detail, and I missed out on both of those.

Mathilde shows us how to do it–we put a tennis ball into the heel to hold the shape, thread the needle, then make weaving stitches across the hole.

I try. I really do, but mine looks like those pictures of spider webs on drugs. The ones teachers show the whole class so they can scare you into thinking all drugs are bad. 'This is a spider making a web after taking speed,' and the web is a total mess and it always made me furious because my regular medicine is pretty much speed and it helps me filter out the crappy white noise.

Spiders have different brains to us, so I had an argument with my teacher Ms Chandler about how it only showed spider brains on drugs, not human brains, because human brains are different and not every human brain is wired the same way and some of us need speed to function so it's stupid saying all drugs are bad, and then Ms Chandler tried to interrupt me and half way through she went pale and realised she'd said something really stupid and she shut up and I felt so much better.

The radio is full of news from the war–not many victories to report, but at least the French troops have secured some place called *Bois de Caillette*. Then an item comes on about the United States senate voting to remain neutral in the war.

'Not for long,' Mari says as she pushes her needle through her sock.

'What do you mean 'not for long'?' Mathilde looks at us.

'It's just the senate,' Luc murmurs. 'The Americans know what's happening here, they won't let us suffer alone.'

Georges and Mathilde shake their heads. Georges says, 'We are alone.'

'I'm sure they'll send lots of troops,' Mari says, then looks at me for backup.

My pulse hammers. I don't know when the Americans joined. 'The Australians are here, they're helping.' They are here, right?

'How do you know this?' Mathilde asks.

This sock I'm darning is unwearable. I remember something the nun said back at the hospital, about sending notices across countries. 'I had a telegram from my cousins,' I start.

'But Marianne and Luc are your cousins,' Mathilde says.

'I mean . . . my other cousins.' I didn't pause too long then, did I?

Marianne says, 'Our American friends will come to our aid. But it's taking a long time because they are so far away.'

'Hmpf!' Georges says. 'The *Boche* used to be our friends too!'

Despite the warmth of the fire, cold dread seeps through me. I am convinced America played some part in the First World War. I wish I knew the answers. I wish I could give Mathilde and Georges some kind of reassurance.

But I can't even give them a decently darned sock.

***

Our chance to get Luc in front of the mirror comes via Georges the next day. As the morning light shines through the kitchen window, Georges looks at Luc's face and points at the downy fuzz on his chin.

'Heh heh! The boy needs to shave!'

The colour in Luc's face drains.

'Come with me, lad,' Georges says.

'No, really, I'll be fine.'

'Heh heh!' Georges gives Luc a friendly slap on the back. He reaches in to a drawer and pulls out a belt and a huge knife.

'Your injured ankle is the least of your problems now,' Marianne laughs at him.

I can't watch. 'He'll cut his face open.'

No sooner has Georges put a small mirror on the table than Luc screams, 'The mirror's all wrong!'

'Hooray! He sees the light!' Marianne says.

Luc's jaw is open in shock as he moves his hands about, left and right.

'Calm down, boy.' Mathilde rubs her hands down the

75

front of her pinafore in that familiar way, a worried expression on her face.

Georges shakes his head. 'I haven't even sharpened the blade!'

'You have to look at this.' Luc reaches for Mathilde. 'There! Look, I move my left hand but the right moves in the mirror. It's wrong.'

'Are you soft in the head?' Mathilde says.

Luc pushes himself away from the table. 'This is definitely not how mirrors work!'

Georges shakes his head. 'He's not ready to shave.'

'Um . . . Mathilde? Georges?' My voice sounds timid. 'Marianne and I also noticed the mirror in your room. We don't think it works properly either. Is it just your mirrors, or is it all of them?'

Mathilde's shoulders rise and fall in a classic Gallic shrug. 'You are such strange children. This is how mirrors work. It's called a projection. It's completely normal.'

'It should be a *reflection*,' Luc says, 'I raise my right arm and in the mirror, it should look like my left is raised.'

It's Georges' turn to shake his head. 'You've given him too many cups of poppy tea, woman. You've addled his brain.'

'I gave him no such thing.'

'I think . . .' Marianne takes Georges by the arm and leads him to a seat, 'we all need to talk. Luc, Inge, we need to tell them the truth.'

My stomach ties itself in knots. This is now my third day off tablets and I can't think straight. I have a headache. I want to cry. I want to pick at that stray thread on the hem of my skirt. I want to itch my foot something terrible.

Marianne looks to Mathilde and says, 'I am being completely honest with you. We are not from around here.'

Thanks, Mari, you've really dropped us in it!

– TEN –

'**I CAN** tell you're not from around here!' Mathilde's forehead creases into lines of ploughed fields.

Marianne clears her throat. 'Luc is my brother. Ingrid is like a sister to us. She really is from Australia. She is living with us as part of an international student exchange visit.'

Mathilde nods but says nothing. I don't believe for a minute she understands us. Did they even have student exchange visits a hundred years ago? I bet they didn't.

Marianne clears her throat. 'We are from the year twenty sixteen. We were all born in the year two thousand.'

Mathilde's jaw drops.

Oh *merde*, the look on her face makes my intestines scrunch up.

'What are you talking about?' Georges' eyebrows dart together.

Luc's got his hands up. 'We really are only sixteen years old. We're not soldiers. We're just kids. The three of us fell through some kind of hole in time. We were doing a role-play of the hundredth anniversary of the *Battle of The Somme*. It happened in July, nineteen sixteen. I mean, it will happen . . . will start to happen. You said it is April, which means *The Somme* begins in three months.

Things are going to get really bad, really soon. You have to get out.'

That's the gist of what he said, anyway. I kind of zoned out in the middle there, what with being so shocked that Marianne and Luc told the truth about when we're from. The air is thick with doubt and simmering anger. I think Georges and Mathilde think we're all crazy.

I think we're crazy.

'Except, for us, *The Somme* happened a century ago. We only know about it through studying history,' Luc says. 'Which is lucky that I have studied so much history so we could warn you about the dangers to come. So you can avoid it.'

'You're all on poppy juice.' Scraping his chair back, Georges rises from the table.

Luc's Adam's apple bobs sharply up and down.

'Please, we're telling the truth.' Marianne's voice sounds thin and panicked. 'We really have come from twenty sixteen. It's the absolute truth.'

'Go to the devil!' Georges says. 'This is a fine way to repay our hospitality. We take you in, give you food and a bed, treat you like family and in return you tell us wild stories.'

'You have to believe us. It is the truth,' Marianne looks to me for backup.

I want to stay out of it because I might make things worse. My brain is off the grid, I don't trust it any more.
Mathilde's eyes are down and her chin wobbles. I feel lower than scum. The poor woman, hasn't she suffered enough?

Luc tries something else. 'Can I tell you what happens, and when it comes true, you will believe us then?'

'I'll believe you're the devil!' Georges says.

'Listen.' Luc starts talking with his hands and I miss the

start of what he says, because his distracting fingers are fluttering about so much. '. . . is coming, and it will begin on July the first, over near the river. Thousands and thousands of soldiers on both sides are going to die. We have some success in liberating Curlu, but for the most part, it achieves little. You have to get out of here, because Amiens isn't safe. Paris is safe, get to Paris.'

Georges spits on the floor. 'Curlu? Never heard of it.'

'It is a few kilometres down the road –'

' –You think we are idiots? If we leave the house, you'll steal everything! You are a pack of lying Gypsies! Get out!'

That's so racist! 'No, please, Georges.' I should keep my mouth shut but I can't help it. 'We really are from the future. The war will be over soon. The Australians are here, and the Americans are coming, but not for a while yet. But it will all be over in three more years.'

'Two more,' Luc corrects me.

'Really? Why am I thinking nineteen nineteen?'

Luc scowls at me. A real scowl. 'Because you don't know your history.' Then he turns to the Gaillards again and his expression is pleading, not provoking. 'Georges, the treaty was signed–will be signed–on the eleventh of November, nineteen eighteen. And we are on the winning side. The Americans and Canadians and the British and the Australians and the New Zealanders have all helped. The Germans are pushed back. The war is over. Will be over.'

'You're mixing up your tenses,' Marianne says.

'You try getting your head around it then!'

Sickness crawls around my stomach. 'I think we're confusing them.'

Georges' eyes narrow. Meanwhile, Mathilde stays in her chair, her eyes downcast. The tip of her chin puckers in pain and her lips quiver.

'We do not mean to upset you,' Marianne says. 'We are as shocked by this as you. It is a lot to take in. We desperately want to go home but we don't even know where to start. But I believe we are here for a reason. Surely it is to warn you. Maybe to warn the whole town to evacuate to safety?'

'Stop, please.' Mathilde's voice cracks. The room falls silent as a tear spills down her cheek.

Watching her hold back emotions is more painful than if she flat out wailed.

'I am so sorry to upset you like this.' I try for the 'dutiful daughter' act. It used to work on Mum, it might work here.

'No more.' Mathilde wipes her face with the back of her hand. 'You are not my beautiful girls. God took them in his wisdom that I don't understand. I thought . . . I thought maybe I had been good and . . . all these years later he had returned you to me. My sweet girls. They would be near your age now.'

Now the tears really come, pouring down Mathilde's face, twisting her mouth into horrible shapes as she tries to go on.

Marianne embraces Mathilde. 'I am so sorry. Your losses are so great. We never meant to hurt you, truly.'

'You still have your sons,' Luc says.

As if that's any consolation. Like the time people used to say to my mum after a miscarriage, 'At least you can get pregnant.'

Georges shakes his head and looks at the ground.

Wiping her face, Mathilde draws breath and pushes her shoulders back.

Somewhere in all this, I've stopped breathing.

'Our sons are dead,' Mathilde says. 'They died in *Ypres* last year. Is that not right, husband?'

Confusion addles my senses. When we'd met Georges at the station, he'd told us to say their sons were doing well. Now Mathilde is saying they're dead?

Georges' eyes rim red. 'Yes, my love. Our sons are dead. All our children are dead.'

I'm going to throw up good and proper this time.

'It feels . . . it feels like I am not real anymore,' Mathilde says. 'When the telegram arrived, I refused the messenger. Maybe . . . I thought if I never read it, it could not be true.'

My vision clouds with heat and I'm going to start blubbering. Luc scratches his face, looking like he might cry as well.

'It is too awful.' Marianne hugs Mathilde. 'When children lose their parents, they are orphans. But there is no word for a parent who loses their children, because it is so unthinkable.'

Mathilde draws a handkerchief from her sleeve and blows noisily. 'You are so very wrong. There is a word. It is a shell. Because that is all I am. A shell with nothing left inside.'

Then Mathilde folds her body in on itself and bawls, howling like a wild animal, as if all that held-back grief has found its way out.

Wiping my face, I wish I could be anywhere but here. Georges moves to Mathilde. The two hold each other, united in grief.

Before I can stop her, Marianne squashes me in a bear hug.

'I'm OK.' I wish she'd stop, but with so much misery in the room, it's also comforting to have someone to hug.

Luc clears his throat. 'I think, maybe we should leave. We've upset you too much.'

I want to help Mathilde but I also want to run from her pain. I'm not cut out for this.

Georges breaks from his wife. 'That may be for the best. I will get you tickets for the train to Paris. The main line is still out, so you'll have to take the branch line.'

Yes, Paris is safer than here if Luc's right about history. And then, once we're safe, we can work out how the heck we're going to get home.

I look to George. 'Will they be proper tickets, so we'll have allocated seats and won't get kicked off?' I don't want a repeat of the last train ride.

'Of course.' Georges is an illustration of confusion.

Luc extends his trembling hand to shake Georges'. 'Thank you,' Luc says. 'And please, for your safety, you should both go to Paris as well. Paris is safe.'

God I hope he's right about that. Because we've been wrong about just about everything else so far.

– ELEVEN –

WE'RE on a steam train again, this time with valid tickets. We're also in the passenger carriage instead of the goods van so things are looking up. Seats to sit on instead of a timber floor. Bread and cheese to snack on instead of chomping down on carrots.

Best of all, we're not wearing uniforms, we're in regular old-timey clothes so we don't stand out in the crowd.

And it's daytime instead of late night.

The train is clean, but the people on it? Not so much. Musty body smells waft around the carriage. The lack of deodorant is only one of the many reasons I desperately want to go home. I want a shower, I want to wear my clothes again and I want to sleep in a proper bed. I miss my friends back home and I miss my Mum.

I also want there to not be a war on. Sure, that list makes me sound selfish but I'm so sick of history. I don't mind studying it, but I sure hate living it. And there are no wars when and where I'm from.

Uh-oh, I just realized I'm wrong. There are wars, but it's been going on so long. Ever since I was born just about. But not directly at home, they're in the Middle East and stuff. There are always wars going on somewhere in the world but . . . I can't think about it or I'll go mad.

'Be grateful it's not high summer,' Marianne whispers to me, wafting her hand in front of her nose.

We're in an open-plan carriage with rows and rows of wooden bench seats. For some reason, I thought we'd be in one of those closed-in carriages with little rooms seating six people. With doors you can close so you can get some peace and quiet. With soft bench seats. Like the ones in those old movies.

Oh dear God there's a live chicken in here crapping on the floor.

We must be in economy class.

From the worry on the other passengers' faces, we're all fleeing the war, headed to Paris for safety, not a holiday. Lots of mothers with broods of children. Hardly any men. They must be in uniform in the trenches then. Every traveller has heavy suitcases; as if they are taking everything they can carry.

Between us, we have one small suitcase, courtesy of Georges and Mathilde. One more thing we took from them. We don't need much. Once we get to Paris, we won't stay long. As soon as Luc thinks of a way to get us home we'll be out of here. I'm open to suggestions from Marianne as well. I wonder if we can find some scientist to help us. Is Einstein around these parts?

Hang on, I don't think he was French.

From his pocket, Luc pulls out a piece of paper. 'I'm going to ask the conductor to remind us when we get to this stop.'

Marianne makes a face. 'I thought we'd go all the way to the terminus?'

'Georges gave it to me. It's a clothing factory just outside Paris, where we can get jobs. I aim to pay the Gaillards back for their hospitality.'

'I don't want to work. I want to go home.' Call me selfish all you want, but I have no intention of getting a job. Not that I'm lazy. I have a part time job at the supermarket near home in Melbourne; I babysit neighbour's kids and do loads of chores. It's just that a temporary job in nineteen sixteen sounds way too much like settling down.

Marianne sounds annoyed too. 'Is this your new plan? We get jobs? Rent an apartment or something? What happened to going home as soon as we could?'

'I don't know.' Luc shrugs.

Lightning-bolt anger spikes me. 'You don't know? Jesus Luc, I thought you had some kind of plan!'

'Please stop using His name –'

'– all right!' I should watch my mouth. I know Mari's sensitive about religious-themed cussing. But this kind of news calls for swearing. The other passengers look at me with disapproval in their eyes. They must have heard me.

They can overhear this as well. 'We are not staying here a minute longer than we have to. We have to get home!'

'Calm down,' Marianne's tone is soothing to me, while she gives Luc a filthy glare. 'We are going home, that is the end of it.'

Luc keeps his voice low. 'You're not seeing the up side of this. We know what is going to happen. We know what to look out for. We'll be fine.'

What? He wants to stay? That was never on the table. Despite being surrounded by people, I don't care who hears me. 'That's not part of the plan. We're getting away from the front, and then we're getting home.'

'We never discussed a timeframe,' Luc says back.

Up yours sideways with an echidna. 'We never talked about staying either.' I'm going right off him. He may have saved our lives that first night by the woodpile, but since then he's changed.

'Yes, I did. When we were in the train, in the goods van, I said it wouldn't be so bad because of,' and here he drops his voice, 'you know . . . we know how this ends.'

'Yeah, it ends badly,' Marianne says.

'Not for us. Listen, we will keep safe, we'll get jobs, pay back the Gaillards, then make proper investments and get out of the stock market in time. We'll have more money than we know what to do with.'

Investing in the bloody stock market? He has completely lost his mind. I want to punch him in the throat. Then strangle him. Then rip his head off. In time with the clacking of the train is a drumbeat in my head: *I want to go home, I want to go home, I want to go home.*

There's no stopping Luc. 'Think about it. Throughout history, people have made immense fortunes, coming up with inventions that are way ahead of their time. Others have somehow missed being involved in massive calamities. Like the people who had tickets for the Titanic and then didn't go. How did they do it?'

I'm struggling too much with fear of the war to be able to think about Luc's theory in any given detail. 'Plenty of people miss boats and planes all the time. It's only later they think it's for a reason.'

Luc splays his palms out. 'We must be here for a reason. Why not take advantage of the situation?'

Mari shakes her head, 'Quite the mercenary, aren't you?'

'Do either of you have any better ideas?'

So many thoughts crash through my head I can't untangle one from the other. My silence gives Luc license to gloat. Everyone else on the train is chatting or coughing or blowing their nose or shushing children. Not forgetting the clucking chicken. I sit in mute shock as the train pulls into a station. Nobody gets off, but more travellers cram on.

Two older men, with official-looking hats step on board, asking for, 'Pie-pye' and 'do-cyu-mo'.

I scrunch my forehead at Mari. 'Papers and documents,' she translates.

OK, it sort of sounded like that, except in French. Whoa, this lot speak French!

Time to hand over my favourite saying. *'Je suis Australien'*.

'Tre byen, documo?' Mister official-in-the-hat asks.

Oh, so he still wants my papers. I shrug and wait for Mari or Luc to say something in French that will save us. Luc says something incredibly fast and Mari whispers to me. 'He says our papers were lost in a fire, after our home was bombed.'

Luc hands them the scribbled note from Georges, along with our tickets.

The men chat with Luc, while Mari whispers English in my ear. 'Many people don't have their documents, because of the bombing. Luc says we are war orphans and we're going to work in a munitions factory to do our duty, even though we are homeless.

'She is a good translator,' one of the men says in English, pointing at Mari. 'You are from Calais, no?'

'Reims, actually.' Mari says, in English for my benefit.

The men make that Gallic shrug and move on to the next people, checking their papers and tickets and whatever else takes their time. The train pulls out of the station and we're heading south once again.

I look at Mari. 'Why would he think we're from Calais?'

'Your guess is as good as mine,' she says.

The day ages towards noon. The sun shines through the windows, heating the carriage like a flame under a soup pot. We stop at every tiny outpost along the way. Each time the carriage gets more crowded. Nobody's getting off the train and I don't blame them. We all want to be as far away from the war as possible.

Luc picks at the scab of our earlier conversation. 'Are you both afraid of work? Is that why you're sulking?'

'Resorting to insults now?' Mari blows her hair out of her eyes, 'While I think paying back Georges and Mathilde is the right thing to do, I would have liked to have been consulted first.'

'So you've come around to my way of thinking.'

'No way,' Mari shoots back. 'But I agree we were an imposition to them and we owe them something.'

I don't exactly agree with tying us down to a job, but if I argue with Mari as well, I'll be cast adrift. 'I agree with Mari sending money to the Gaillards. But Luc, you can't just go around making decisions for all of us. We have to decide together.'

Luc snorts derision. 'What you're both saying is, we should reimburse them, yes?'

'Yes.' Mari says and I nod.

'Then you both agree with me. So what's the problem?'

It's probably for the best Mari is sitting between Luc and me, because I would have slapped that smug grin off his face.

'Stop enjoying yourself so much.' Mari says to him.

Luc throws his head back and laughs. It earns us strange looks from other passengers. How dare he see the funny side of this? I'm scared out of my skin and he thinks it's all some monumental joke.

The train grinds to a stop at Saint-Gratien. 'This is us,' Luc says, checking his paper again.

We are the only three passengers to leave the train. I cannot forgive Luc for not letting us go all the way to Paris and working out some kind of plan together. I feel even more out of control than before, and that's saying something. Resentment takes hold, and it's not just because I want to see the sights of Paris, either in this century or ours. I truly am desperate to get home, but I'm stuck with Luc who wants to stay and play.

Once the soot from the train clears, the air smells fresh. Different too, like something damp and organic. I'm tempted to think it's mown grass, but lawnmowers probably haven't been invented yet. On the other hand, my armpits are far from fresh. 'If you want to make money on an invention, Luc, hurry up and make deodorant.'

'I don't think you're too bad.' He winks at me.

He's flirting with me now? How am I supposed to stay angry with him when he does this to me?

We take the footbridge that spans the railway lines below. As we reach the top, I look down the line where I imagine Paris might be. The landscape rolls away from us, rumpled like an unmade bed. 'I can't see the Eiffel Tower.'

Marianne looks hard. 'We are probably too far away. Maybe there are buildings in the way?'

'That's a shame.' I can't help being a tourist. I want to see the tower. What's the point of coming all the way to France and not seeing Paris and the tower, right?

Luc stops and turns his sights towards the city. 'That's weird. It can't be tall buildings in the way. They're not that tall yet.'

'Trees then?' Mari suggests.

'Maybe we're looking in the wrong direction? That way is south, isn't it?' Reading maps is not my strong suit.

'It must be a perspective thing. I know it's there,' Luc says.

'I always thought it was a movie cliché,' I have another look, but it's fruitless. 'You know, everyone in Paris has a view of the tower from their hotel window.'

Luc grins at me and . . . he *is* flirting with me. Lousy timing, mate.

A sign on the bridge says *'sortie'* with an arrow. I remember that means exit. Looking around, all the road and shop signs look like they're in proper French, not English, like they were at Amiens. Maybe Luc was right about doing that to confuse the enemy. I can't hear any bombs or guns, so maybe we're a long way from the front?

Maybe we're safe?

'They nearly pulled it down, did you know that? The tower I mean,' Luc says to nobody in particular as we walk towards the road and the town proper.

OK, I'll bite. 'Really?'

'Eiffel designed it to be dismantled. At first people hated it, but then—and here is the clever part—such a tall tower could intercept German radio transmissions. It is helping us win the war right now.'

He really, *really* loves his history.

'I'm going to patent wheels for suitcases,' Mari says.

Luc jumps on the comment. 'Aha! You are thinking of staying?'

'Merely wishing out loud. Don't get excited.'

Walking down the village streets, we pass a row of shops where people are strolling around, their arms laden with baskets of groceries. They seem more at ease than the villagers in Amiens.

Some are even enjoying a cafe-au-lait at the tables in the sunshine.

What does strike me as similar to Amiens—there are no fatties here either.

I mentally slap my forehead. Of course people are slim. Hardly anyone has a car so everyone has to walk everywhere. That would really get your daily steps up.

All the shops are open and trading, none of the windows are covered in newspaper. I half expect to hear a piano accordion playing.

'You'd barely know there was a war on,' Marianne says what I'm thinking.

In a few blocks, we reach the factory gates and walk in, heading straight to the foreman's entrance. Luc hands over the letter of introduction to a man wearing a heavy blue overcoat.

He looks about thirty. '*Bonjour*!' he says to us, before rabbiting on in French. He points to the patch above his pocket with his first name, *Henri*, embroidered on it. The smile he gives us is disarming, goofy even. His eyes don't look so sharp. Maybe the embroidery is for his benefit, not ours?

He looks naggingly familiar, but I can't place him. Which is only going to bug me all the more. Like the way I can't enjoy a movie until I know who the actor is and what else I've seen him or her in.

Better not stare at him, he's freaking me out.

Mari translates for me. 'He is asking if we have any work experience.'

I deliberately stand back a little way so Henri doesn't ask me any direct questions. There's something odd about this bloke and I don't want him to catch me staring at him. In this instance, it might be easier to let Luc do all the talking.

***

We'll be doing second shift, which begins at two o'clock in the afternoon and finishes at eleven in the evening. We'll get a half hour for dinner at six, then a quarter-hour break at nine. Really civilized from the sounds of things.

Henri gives us a quick tour ahead of starting. The bathrooms are space-aged compared to the Gaillard household. Proper toilets in cubicles and basins with hot and cold running water.

'Hot water . . .' Marianne turns the tap to full and plunges her hands under the flow. 'It's heavenly!'

Above the sinks, polished steel panels stand in for mirrors. They're just as bonkers as the one in the Gaillard's house, what with our movements going the wrong way and all that. I'll just have to get used to them.

At the end of the row of toilets I see a dispensing machine. 'Mari, look at this. It's got sanitary pads.'

'What?' Mari steps closer for a better look. 'Only one centime each. What a life saver!'

Just in case we don't get home before *The English Arrive*, at least I won't have to wear the rags!

Something nags at me. 'I didn't think these were invented so early?'

'Yeah . . .' Marianne's voice fades a little. 'I didn't . . .' She shakes her head as a confused look crosses her face. 'This is a modern factory, for its time, but . . . this dispenser seems way out of place. I must ask Luc if he knows about them.'

'Euw, please don't!'

'I meant dispensing machines in general, not what's in them.'

'Oh.' I giggle with relief.

Henri and Luc are waiting for us when we come out. The solid factory noise chimes with my brain and it's working for me. It's helping me think straight, or it's blocking out my usual extraneous thoughts. Don't know; not going to think about it. All I know is that for the first time since falling thought time, the usual twenty-seven-million apps all open at the same time in my brain are switched off.

The tour continues to the dining hall, where Henri shows off the rows of tables and bench seats, as if he'd built them. Maybe he did? There's a long galley kitchen and several *bains-marie* warming dishes. They're empty for now, but that doesn't stop me fantasizing about what will fill them at meal times.

What a fabulous place. Bathroom on site, and they fed you. If I wasn't so angry with Luc for railroading us into taking this job, I'd thank him.

Henri opens the heavy doors to the factory floor. Machinery buzzes in my ears. It no longer matters that I can't understand Henri's French, because now I can't even hear him over the rattling and hammering and disjointed hums and sudden whirring.

I love it. The extra noise is giving me a break from processing anything.

Rows of sewing stations, filled with dozens of boys and girls who all look about our age, pushing pale blue material through sewing machines.

'I haven't done this before.' Mari has to say it loudly so I can hear her over the din.

In the distance, an older woman, maybe thirty, waves at Henri and walks towards us, pulling a set of yellow plugs out of her ears. A scarf smothers most of her hair, but blonde wisps escape out the sides. Her name is embroidered on her jacket.

At first she too speaks French, then she notices Mari translating for me and leaps straight into English. 'I am Valerie. I supervise the afternoon shift. Have you worked before?'

We all looked a bit sheepish, saying things like:

'No.'

'Not really.'

'Uh-uh.'

Valerie gives us a beaming smile and says, 'With your curling hair, Ingrid, you'd get caught in the machines. We'll start you on the cutting tables instead. Come with me.' Then she turns to Henri, rattles off instructions to him and turns back to us. 'Henri will take care of your belongings. You may collect them at the end of your shift.'

Instinct tells me Henri will paw through our stuff.

'Come with me,' Valerie reaches into her pocket to produce more yellow earplugs. They are tactile and spongelike, but I can't tell what they're made of. Squashing them into my ears, they work well enough to block Valerie's voice, but not the din of machinery. With the way my brain's been *unhelping* me, I'm glad the droning factory noise is still getting through.

On we walk, past rows of workers wearing scarves like Valerie's, less as a fashion statement and more as a safety feature to secure their hair back. Some of the women looked up and give us a quick nod or smile, but the rest are far too busy.

Towards the back of the cacophonous hall are more workers, with rolls and rolls of fabric. They're spreading the fabric out over broad tables. Everyone is wearing overcoats with their names embroidered on them.

Valerie gives us a quick demonstration. 'Always roll the bolts of cloth out on the underside, and bring the edge of the fabric in line with the edge of the table like this. Take your template and place it over the fabric.' She picks up a large metal shape and puts it on the cloth. 'Line the arrows on the template with the weave of the fabric. This is very important, our soldiers need to be able to run and move. The fabric must move with them. They cannot fight the Germans if they are fighting their uniforms as well.'

Valerie traces the template edges with a thin wafer of chalk. Then she takes a smaller template and places it inside the first chalk outline, creating a second outline within.

Valerie looks satisfied. 'You see here, we make an extra two centimetres for sewing strong seams.' I've never made clothes before, but the cutting out stage doesn't look so hard. At least they don't have me darning socks.

Valerie goes on, 'Placing the templates in this way uses the least amount of fabric, while also allowing our brave soldiers maximum comfort.'

Comfort? This is the same blue wool material we wore in the trenches. It itched and scratched and drove me insane.

'Ingrid and Marianne, you know what to do now. If you need help, ask one of the ladies here. Luc, follow me to the laundry.'

'Laundry?' Worry is written all over him.

'Of course.' Valerie speaks as if he's five years old. 'All the cloth must be washed before we can make the uniforms. Otherwise the moment our men get wet, their clothes will shrink.'

Marianne looks to Valerie and says, 'You have to wash wool in cold water, don't you?'

'Of course!' Valerie gives us frustrated glances but I know where Mari is going with this. Luc will be up to his armpits in cold water, while we are warm and dry in here.

Please, please let this job be so awful it will put Luc off wanting to stay.

– TWELVE –

I DON'T dare say this out loud in case Luc thinks I'm enjoying living in the past, but life is kind of good here at the factory. We're safe from the war and the meals in the food hall are hot and filling. Over the past few weeks, my job of marking out the uniform patterns has become easier. We're only doing jackets and coats. There's something a little zen about the repetitive task. The noise calms my brain too.

I don't know how they're doing it, but we have hot showers and soap in the communal bathrooms here. There are even locks on the doors.

On the downside, there is no shampoo or conditioner so my hair is seriously knotted. Thank goodness I can hide it all under a scarf. At some point I'm going to have to try something. Maybe warm olive oil might help? Coupled with the vinegar I splash under my armpits every afternoon, I'll smell like salad dressing.

All the while I can't help wondering how or if time is passing back in our own proper time. Have my parents flown to France to look for me? Is my picture all over the internet? Please let Mum or Dad pick a decent selfie. They want people to want to find me, don't they?

Judging by the huge smile on Luc's face as he eats with us, he's loving every minute of this time travel experience. To think, the reason I joined Luc and Marianne in the trenches that day was because I fancied seeing Luc in uniform.

Yeah but no. The novelty of re-enacting history has well and truly worn off. Every day in nineteen sixteen feels the same. Work, eat during the breaks here in the food hall, then return to our dorm for some sleep. The factory provides the dorm and the food and the work clothes, deducting twenty per cent of our pay for the privilege.

But we're a long way from the war so we're relatively safe. Now if Mari and I can just get Luc interested in working out a way home, rather than simply working here, we might get somewhere.

Between bites of her dinner, Marianne scratches at her tummy. She makes me itchy just looking at her. Now I'm scratching my belly. No, Luc, don't you start too.

'Three dots in a row?' He asks.

'Yeah, and plenty of them.'

'Is it chicken pox?' Marianne asks, digging her nails in.

'Can't be,' I say. 'I had a jab for that. And chicken pox is more like a random rash. These look like bites, because they line up?'

Luc looks at me and winks. 'You show me yours, I'll show you mine.'

'It's fine, really.' Why is he looking at me like that?

'Here.' Marianne pulls up my shirt to show the spots on my tummy.

'Bedbugs,' Luc says.

'A-whatta?' I could have sworn he just said –

'Bed. Bugs.' The grin on his face shows how much he's enjoying this. 'Little things that sleep with you and suck your blood in the night. It is nothing personal. Everyone has them. Look, I have them too.' He unbuttons his shirt and shows me a series of red bites across his chest.

Mouth turning dry, I manage to say, 'Well, I don't want them.' Itchy heat takes hold across the back of my neck. Time to change the subject. 'Have we earned enough to pay the Gaillards back yet?'

I've been giving Mari all my money because I don't trust Luc. He'd do something silly like invest it, or some other stupid long-term thing, while Mari and I are on the same page—we want out.

'Nearly,' Mari says. 'A few more weeks ought to do it.'

A few more weeks of being eaten alive while I sleep? So revolting.

Luc laughs as he buttons himself up. 'We have the day off tomorrow. I thought we might get the train into Paris.'

Ordinarily, I might enjoy the day slobbing about in bed, but not if revolting creatures are eating me. Spending a day walking around Paris with Luc and Marianne could be fun. At least I'll get to see the tower, right?

***

Soot, steam and ash fly everywhere as the train pulls in to the station. We walk towards the Quai Branly as it curves along the Seine River. The vintage cars and elegant clothes make me feel like I've walked onto a movie set. Mari and I can't help looking, pointing and sometimes giggling at the women's costumes. The hats are gorgeous! Some are elaborate caps that hug their owner's heads, others are enormous umbrellas of fabric resting on vast sweeps of hair curled underneath. Considering nobody has any hair product in this era, hats are a brilliant idea.

Mari and I only have scarves. I'm thinking about

holding a few centimes back from our Gaillard fund to buy a hat. No, wait, stop thinking like that. We don't need hats because we won't be here for long enough.

'Everyone is so elegant, so beautiful,' Mari says, 'They're not rushing anywhere either, taking their time. You'd never know there was a war on.'

Ahead of us, Luc stops abruptly. 'It's not possible.'

I don't know what he's on about.

'It's not here.' He scratches at his head. Hopefully a sign of frustration and not lice. I don't want lice powder again, it stinks.

'What are you looking for?' Mari asks.

'It has to be here.' Luc looks left and right, looks back the way we came and starts breathing noisily. His face has dropped two shades, like he's going to hurl.

'If you tell us, we might be able to help you find it,' Mari says.

Luc rubs the side of his forehead. 'The Eiffel Tower. It should be right here!'

Whoa! What?

We are standing on the edge of a vast expanse of parkland. Just ahead of us is the Pont d'Iéna. Sick dread spreads through me. It looks like the green lawns of Paris, the one you see on all the post cards. The one with the great big sky-punching tower down the end. How can we miss something as big as the Eiffel Tower? I'm looking around as well. Nausea spreads through me the more I try to find it and fail.

'Has it been built yet?' Marianne asks.

Luc glares at her. 'Yes it has been built! It was finished in eighteen eighty-nine!'

Marianne gives an indignant huff. 'I'm sorry I don't know everything about history!'

Luc pales and swallows hard.

Mari keeps going. 'It's OK, isn't it? I mean, we're

probably in the wrong place and it's back that way.' She waves her hand in another direction.

She must be right. Paris isn't as crowded as it is in the future, so there's more open space, right?

'It should be right here!' Luc drags his fingers through his hair.

Fear worms through me.

'You two don't get it, do you?' Luc says.

I think I do. That's why I feel sick even though Mari doesn't have a clue. Yet.

'The tower had the first radio transmissions,' Luc says. 'The army sent messages to the frontlines. Both in this war and the next. It kept lines open. They intercepted messages from the Germans and knew what they were planning. Without that –' He throws his hands up in hopelessness.

Panic burns the back of my throat.

'Maybe . . .' Marianne looks confused and lost.

'Maybe what?' Luc is ready to pick a fight.

'Don't get snippy with me.' Mari shoots back. 'I'm trying to think. Maybe we're in the wrong place.'

Red blotches grow on Luc's face. 'Do you think I am so stupid that I don't even know where the Eiffel Tower is?'

Marianne sticks her hands on her hips. 'Do you really want me to answer that?'

'Stop fighting, please!' I can't stand it. 'We're all tired. We just need a moment to think and work this out. We just need to calm down and stop panicking and let our brains relax and come up with an answer.'

'The Eiffel Tower is missing. The Eiffel Tower for God's sake!' He smacks himself on the forehead and staggers backwards. Every breath he takes seems slow and deliberate. When he speaks again, his words sound stilted and strained. 'It all makes sense now. The road signs in English. Mirrors not reflecting properly, the way old Georges said the war started in nineteen twelve instead of nineteen fourteen. Even the earplugs at the factory are way ahead of their time.'

He stares us down to help us absorb the full horror. My brain has raced ahead to the conclusion already, but I don't want to think it. I'm going to wait for Luc to say it, because I don't want to.

'We're not just in the wrong time. We're in the wrong freaking world!'

My bones turn to rubber bands and the ground races upwards. My legs fold underneath me. The street trees turn blurry as tears ruin everything. 'I can't take it. I just can't take one more thing going wrong. I'm going to shut my eyes and when I open them again, I'll be back in my own time, in my own bed.'

'Why must you upset her like that?' Marianne crouches down to me, hugging my shoulders. 'Luc's playing a joke. But it's not funny.'

'He's not,' I blubber. This is why nothing made sense. Proper sense. Because Luc is right, and I noticed it at first, what with the road signs and everyone speaking English. We're not simply stuck in time, we're stuck on some kind of 'I Can't Believe It's Not France' and everything is completely mental.

'Mari, this is not a joke,' Luc says. 'I am in just as much shock as you.'

Now it's Mari's turn to wobble. Her fear sends aftershocks through my shoulders. 'You could have found a nicer way to say it.'

'I am still trying to process it myself.'

'Luc . . .' Mari's voice trails off. 'When you say, 'the wrong world' what exactly do you mean?'

'I don't think we fell through time in a straight line. Or

whatever you do when you fall through time. I'm hardly the expert. We're in some kind of alternate world where the tower isn't here any more and . . .' His voice wavers off and he drags his hands through his hair again. 'For all we know in this world Germany could win the war.'

I want to scream but there's no breath in me to do that.

Luc noisily sucks in air. 'We need to find out what happened to the tower. Maybe there's something in the gardens that might give us a clue.'

'In case you failed to notice dear brother, Ingrid is in no shape to walk.'

'Fine, I will carry her.'

In my scrambled emotional state, the last thing I want is for Luc to view me as a cripple. 'It's OK, I can get up.' Although I don't know if I can. "PS, I was right about the road signs and you ignored it. That was such a massive clue and you brushed it off, and I was right all along.'

'Yes, you were right, I was ignoring you.' Luc holds his hand out. 'Here, let me help.' His voice is all kindness, which only makes me feel worse on the inside. 'You were the first to spot things that were wrong. The road signs, and the Gaillards speaking English should have been our first clue that this was not the real France. I'm sorry for not listening to you more.'

It's one shock after another today. Before I can put two words together, he's got his arms around my shoulders and is guiding me back to my feet. 'There you are.'

How can he be so nice to me after I've been so mean to him? OK, not mean exactly, but I've hardly been as friendly as I could have been since he told us he wanted to stay here. Because I've been so scared. It's hard to be nice when all you can think about is how scared you are.

Not that I can get my thoughts straight. It's too quiet here, my brain has all the apps open again. I need factory noises to shut them off.

The strangest out-of-body feeling takes hold as he walks me through the parkland. As if this were all happening to someone else and I'm only an observer. He smells like a mixture of sweat and something acidic. Probably vinegar. Maybe that's me?

The gardens are packed with trees and shrubs of all kinds. So much greenery calms me enough to start thinking about how much trouble we're in. And if there's any way of getting out of it.

I thought being stuck in time was bad enough, now we're stuck in some other world that looks just like ours but isn't? I'd love to be able to faint right now and wake up when Luc and Marianne have figured it all out.

Our boots crunch on the gravel paths beneath us. Marianne leads me towards a bench seat in the shade and we sit down. Yes, sitting in the shade. If I close my eyes, maybe I'll fall asleep and they can wake me when it's over.

'You both stay there and I'll have a look around,' Luc says.

'After all this, we're still letting him take charge?' I ask.

'I'm only letting him think he's in charge,' Mari says. She points to the other side of the path. There's a sculpture made from beams of riveted iron. At the base is a picture frame. I can't see it properly from here, but I can sort of make out the image of a pointy tower.

Thinking back to the day our train pulled into town, I remember we looked towards Paris, hoping for a glimpse of the tower. 'He said the public hated it and they were going to pull it down . . .' Every muscle in my body hums with fear and anticipation. My joints feel buzzy and out of control. This is exactly the right place for the tower, and I have to face the reality. It really isn't here any more.

Luc reads the inscription aloud for our benefit. 'About

these gardens stood the Eiffel Tower, from eighteen eighty-nine until nineteen oh-nine. It was dismantled and sold to –' He charges off towards some bushes.

'What's he do –'

We hear retching noises.

'– Never mind.'

Marianne stands up and walks towards the monument.

'Does it matter what the rest of it says, Mari?' I ask. 'It's not going to bring it back.'

'It says they sold it to Germany for one franc,' Marianne says. 'On condition Germany pay for the dismantling and removal. It now stands in Bismarckstrasse, Berlin.' She twirls her finger to the side of her head. 'It's all gone lulu.'

After wiping his hands on tufts of grass, Luc walks back and reads the monument again. No amount of reading will change the facts though.

Horrible thoughts assail me. If France used the tower to monitor radio transmissions, like Luc said, does that mean Germany is doing the same amount of monitoring back to us? I mean, France?

It's the perfect cluster bomb of bad news.

A fresh shiver takes hold as the next fear steps in. Luc's transformation from confident know-all to scared little boy has happened so fast I can hardly process it. Ever since we fell through time, he's enjoyed himself. Far too much. Reliving history seemed second nature to him because he knew it all. Now we're all just as scared as each other.

It was fine when it was only me being scared. Scared is my default position. Maybe I let Luc take charge because it meant I could be scared without having to solve anything? I left it to Luc, therefore he could deal with things while I turned to jelly.

Now he's just as freaked as Mari and me.

Amazing how things can get so much worse when you're not paying attention.

Mari asks Luc, 'Why would they sell the Eiffel Tower to our enemies?'

Luc shakes his head. 'I don't think we were enemies at the time. France and Germany used to be allies. Maybe it was a friendship offering?'

'But why Germany of all places?' she asks.

Luc sticks his fists on his hips and turns on the sarcasm. 'I'm sorry, I only know the history of our world, not this one as well!'

'It must be why we're here. We have to fix it so France wins.' Mari says.

Luc scoffs. 'Then we should have arrived a heck of a lot earlier than this.'

An uneasy quiet descends as we retreat into ourselves, trying to digest how messed up everything is. I chew on the skin beside my fingernails. Marianne hugs her arms to her body and nibbles on her lower lip. Luc runs his hands through his hair, then scratches at his neck. His nails leave red lines on his skin.

Gusts of wind rattle the leaves and bring with it the smell of freshly baked bread. My stomach rumbles in anticipation. 'I wonder if they've invented panini yet?' Totally inappropriate but I'm hungry again.

'Stop thinking about food. Start thinking about ways to get home,' Luc says.

Marianne's eyebrows shoot up. 'Praise be to God! You want to go home. Thank you for finally listening to us.'

If Luc wants to go home, it's surely good news. But it also means we are in way more trouble than I could have imagined.

Confident Luc is gone. Scared Luc has taken his place and it terrifies me.

How long have we been sitting here? Time messes with my head. It could be hours, it could be minutes. We're numb from shock. How are we going to get home? We've wasted so much time already without even making the beginnings of an exit plan.

At least Luc's come round to our way of thinking. Shame it took something as massive as the Eiffel Tower not being where it should to get him on our side.

Every time I think of the mess we're in, the answer feels further away. We're in the wrong time, in the wrong universe. Even if we could get off this one, how do we know we'll land back in the right one?

An hour or a minute passes. Luc appears with hot toasted panini and I could kiss him. I had no idea the shops were even open. The panini is delicious. Mine has chicken and parsley and melted brie. Divine doesn't even come close to describing it. We sit for a while, eating quietly and not saying much. We're all dumbstruck from the shock. Clearly not shocked enough to put me off eating though. Would you look at that? Mine's all gone.

While Luc and Marianne finish theirs, my mind jumps from one thing to another as I look at the leftover foundation beams of what used to be the Eiffel Tower. Every now and then I can focus. Now is one of those times, because something pulls all those disparate ideas together and makes something clear in my head.

We might never get home. But we are going to bloody well try. We're going to try everything we can think of and not give up. It won't be easy. In fact, it will probably be terrifying. But we're going to do it, and do it together. I'm done with safe. I'm done with being a passenger. I'm done with hiding in history. We are going home, even if I have to drag Luc and Marianne kicking and screaming all the way with me.

– THIRTEEN –

NOW that I've made up my mind about what we need to do, I can relax and digest lunch and we can have a bit of a think about Operation Get Home.

In my mind, I can see the Eiffel Tower where it should be. It's such a recognisable landmark, I can't believe they didn't love it enough to keep it.

My mind wanders to that scene in that old Superman movie that Mum loved so much. The guy in it was adorkable. There was a bomb on the Eiffel Tower's elevator and Lois Lane was somehow stuck underneath the elevator or something. My Mum's favourite movie had the same actor as Superman in it. He travelled through time and –

Whoa! 'I have an idea.' My heart rate bounces as Luc and Marianne give me their complete attention. They're looking at me with so much hope. Oh dear. Maybe it's not such a good idea? But it's the only one I have so it'll have to do.

At least until I can come up with something else.

'I saw this old movie, *Somewhere In Time*. This guy goes back fifty or eighty years or something to meet this woman, and he gets there by really believing in it. Stop laughing at me.'

'I am not laughing,' Luc says, failing to control his features. 'But it sounds a bit silly.'

'Hear her out!' Marianne says as she finishes her last bite.

I feel stupid for mentioning it but it's all I have. 'It was kind of like our situation. In the movie, the guy was wearing completely authentic clothes for the time period he was going to. He hypnotized himself or went into some kind of trance and when he woke up, he was in the past.'

'That's because it was a movie, Ingrid, not real life,' Luc says. He still has a quarter panini left but he folds it into a serviette and bins it.

'I know that. But think about it, we were wearing authentic clothing when it happened to us. Maybe if we made ourselves some modern clothes, we could do some self-hypnosis and get back to our year. See, in the movie, the guy didn't realize he had a modern coin in his pocket. He pulled it out and saw the date on it and he got sucked back to his own time again.'

'Yeah. In the movie.' Luc shakes his head.

My hands clench in frustration. 'Sorry for trying to help!'

'I would like to give it a try,' Marianne says. 'We work in a clothing factory. We are getting good at making clothes. We will get fabric, we will make our modern clothes and see what happens.'

'Using material from nineteen sixteen?' Luc asks.

'Cotton is still cotton. We should be able to find some. I like Ingrid's idea. I vote we give it a shot,' Marianne says.

It's impossible to hold back my smile. If this works, we'll be home in no time.

A few mornings later, the three of us gather in the dorm room I share with Mari. It's not much. There are two single beds and a little basin in the corner for washing our face. The floor is timber boards with an old rug on the space between our beds. There's a wood heater in the middle of the room with a long metal tube taking the smoke up through the ceiling and out to the sky. If we add enough wood to the heater we can cook biscuits on top.

When it cools down at night and the flames go out, the metal clunks and clanks and things scuttle down. I think the scuttling is coals and soot.

Could be mice.

Hope not.

Boys aren't allowed in the girls' dorm, so we're being extra quiet as we sneak Luc in here so the three of us can think our way back to modern times.

The problem with extra quiet is that all my brain-apps come on, so it's even harder to focus. I'm supposed to be meditating soon.

God help us.

We look like castaways. I've fashioned a pair of cut-off shorts from leftovers, and a baggy t-shirt. I'm also wearing a pair of snug-fitting cotton underpants I made myself. They are so comfortable I want to show them off. Except Luc is here so I won't. Shoes, on the other hand, are completely beyond my abilities, so I'm barefoot.

Loads of people go barefoot in our day.

There's a vaguely fishy smell in here, so I tuck my feet underneath me thinking it must be me.

Marianne is wearing a denim skirt and a cotton vest, worn over a cotton singlet. She looks like she's stepped out of

Mum's high school photos.

Luc has cut a pair of dungarees into long shorts. He is wearing a plain white tee shirt and a look of absolutely no confidence.

Marianne shoots him a dirty look. 'Thanks for making the effort.'

Luc shrugs, 'It won't work.'

'Well, if that is your attitude.' Marianne makes scoffing sounds.

'It is silly. Just look at us,' Luc says.

'Only because you do not want to try,' Mari shoots back.

I can't stand it when they bicker like this. Sure it's a symptom of the stress we're under, but when they fight, we never get anywhere.

But we have to do this together. We arrived together, we're leaving together. That has to be how it works. And if this doesn't work, then we're going to keep right on trying until we make it.

To think I'd spent years wishing I had a sister or a brother to play with! If I'd had a sibling, this is how things would have turned out. Fighting. Teasing. A constant source of irritation. The occasional nice moment of friendship that hardly seems worth it.

'I also made this.' It's show and tell time. I've got a tablet of wood, painted black to look like a mobile phone. I went so far as to dig a slot in the base with a screwdriver to look like the recharge jack.

'Take my photo.' Marianne plays along, putting her hands under her chin to pose.

I hold put my head next to hers, hold the phone out and we take a pretend selfie. A prelfie?

Marianne laughs. 'That is so clever, I wish I'd thought of that.'

'Can I see?' Luc's face brightens as he turns the wooden phone over in his hands. 'That's very good.'

I feel ridiculously pleased at this small dose of praise.

'I made sashimi.' Marianne unwraps a napkin to reveal small ingots of rice with raw fish on top.

Thank goodness it's not my feet making that smell after all.

The Japanese-style food looks authentic, the kind of modern snack we might be eating if we were back home.

Luc's top lip pushes up so high in disgust it nearly covers his nostrils.

Marianne's face crumples in defeat. 'But I could only find dried sardines. I had to soak them for ages to plump them up and get all the salt off.'

I feel guilty for not being more grateful. 'Sorry Mari. It looks like the real thing, and that's what counts right? You did a great job. It's exactly what we need.'

Luc's voice sounds funny, as if he's blocked his nose from the inside. 'And it's not as if we have to eat it.'

True but tactless. 'What did you bring then?'

He unfolds some paper. 'I have here the entire team from France's two thousand and eighteen world cup win.'

My brows clamp downwards in confusion. 'But we're going back to two thousand and sixteen.'

'I know!' He looks pleased with himself. 'But there's nothing wrong with a bit of wishful thinking!'

'You're being stupid!' Marianne crosses her arms over her chest.

'Says the girl who made stinky fish!'

'Shut up! At least I'm trying!' Marianne flings a chunk of rice at Luc. Straight after that she launches herself at him, arms making windmills. Luc puts his hands up in defence but doesn't hit back. Instead, he laughs loudly, which only makes Marianne more furious.

I'm screaming at them, 'Stop fighting! For God's sake!' Everything is falling apart. We have to be united in this or we don't stand a chance.

Also, someone will hear us and wonder what a boy's voice is doing in a girls' dorm and we'll be in trouble or something.

With a grunt, Luc pushes Marianne away. 'You fight like a girl.'

Immediately Marianne throws herself back at Luc, slapping and screaming at him.

Everything is turning to crap. I launch myself between the two of them. With Luc's help we push Mari back.

Keeping my voice low, I hiss at them, 'Both of you calm down. Seriously!'

'He started it,' Marianne protests.

'I don't care!' Only now do I notice my splayed palm is still pressed on Luc's chest. His warm skin radiates through to mine. The thumping of his heart behind his ribs makes a mockery of his nonchalant attitude. Good. He's just as scared as we are. For some strange reason, I kind of admire that.

'You can take your hand off me now,' Luc says.

'Oh.' Oops. Red-hot embarrassment charges up my neck. Time to stay focused. Or get focussed I guess. 'Yes, of course. Let's get started.'

Luc says, 'I suppose we all hold hands and say 'om' or something.'

Time to be honest. I have no idea how we're supposed to proceed. Do we meditate into a trance? We just have to believe it. Maybe if we hold hands and shut our eyes . . . I put my hands out for Ingrid and Luc to take. A long second ticks by before their hands slip into mine. Mari gives me a squeeze of support. Luc's fingers grip the very tip of mine. As if he's going along with us, but only begrudgingly. Hooray, Luc is taking Mari's hand as well. The circle is complete.

'This is will not work,' Luc says.

I wish he'd stop crushing our spirits like that.

'If you don't want to try, you can always stay here in nineteen sixteen in whatever France this is.' It's a total bluff. He must know we wouldn't leave him behind.

Marianne makes a loud 'tisking' sound and glares at him.

'Fine, whatever,' he says.

'OK, um, obviously I've never done this before. But we may as well give it a shot. We arrived here dressed in authentic clothing, which added to the . . . um . . . authenticness of everything.' The way Luc looks so intently at me makes me forget things. Like words.

One moment he's flirting with me, the next minute he's shutting me down. I don't get it.

Marianne picks up my loose threads. 'We are wearing clothes that remind us of our time, and we have the phone, the food and the football team to help us stay focused on our real time.'

'Yes.' It's easier to go on if I look at Mari and ignore the way Luc is adjusting his hand to take mine fully in his. 'What we need to do, is close our eyes and see ourselves back home.'

Marianne looks up. 'Home as in France, or your home in Australia?'

A pang of homesickness hits me. I miss my friends so much. 'Uh . . . France, of course. I mean, we should all be thinking of the same place . . . so . . .' It's a sure sign of nervousness when I end my sentences with a wavering 'so'.

'Let's get on with it then.' Luc's tone changes, as if he's in command and we are the ones playing along. Does this mean he thinks this has a good chance of working?

'Shut your eyes.' He says. 'Picture yourselves in the lounge room. We're playing 'tendo, eating chocolate with pop rocks in it and updating our Instagram accounts.'

Behind my closed eyes, I imagine the enjoyable scene. Lounging about, loads of free time and not doing very much at all. Free time, now there's a concept. We've barely had any since we got here. Just the day out in Paris and look where that got us?

Luc's voice drifts into my thoughts. 'We are feeling relaxed and happy and everything is as it should be.' Contrary to his words, he tightens his grip on my hand. It makes my heart race faster.

Relaxed is the very last thing I'm feeling, but to say otherwise would kill the mood we're creating. 'This feels right,' I say, willing my body to calm the hell down. 'I can smell panini with cheese and tomato.' It's not the slightest bit true, not with the fishiness wafting in my direction.

'It's nice to be home,' Marianne says.

This is going so well, my body actually starts to feel lighter. What a beautiful, positive experience we're sharing.

Luc continues, 'OK, I'm going to count backwards from three. When I finish counting, we're all going to open our eyes and find ourselves back home, as if none of this ever happened. Three, two, one, open your eyes.'

With trepidation, I peek around the room.

Luc has an unreadable expression.

A tear runs down Marianne's face and her chin crinkles as if she is about to burst into a big sooky howl.

– FOURTEEN –

'**I KNEW** it wouldn't work,' Luc drops our hands and stands up.

Marianne wipes her eyes.

The bottom has fallen out of my world. I wasn't confident in the first place, but during our session I felt *something* different.   'Maybe we need to send more money to the Gaillards? And a note begging them to leave Amiens so they can be –'

Luc crosses his arms. 'It's not about the money, OK?'

Why is he so angry with me? Like this is all my fault?

'Then why didn't it work?' Mari looks crushed.

'Because it's stupid!'

Thanks Luc. I'm crushed too.

Mari argues, 'You were not taking it seriously. I knew you would screw it up.'

'Please, guys, don't start fighting again. We're all terrified but arguing will get us nowhere.'

It's another miracle, because they stop trading insults. Then Luc looks at me and says, 'We gave it a try, it didn't work. We'll have to think of another way to get home, that's all.' He's transitioned into problem-solver mode, which should be a good thing. It's a scary thing too. I'm kind of hoping there is some way of getting home that we've overlooked. Maybe I will have to harden up and face the truth, that our only way back is the way we came.

Luc takes his 'modern' gear off and grabs his antique shirt. 'Got any other ideas?'

Who knew the sight of Luc with his shirt off would turn my mouth dry? In contrast, my palms are damp. 'I don't know yet. But . . . we'll keep working on it. This is just a setback. We're going to keep trying, right?'

Marianne says, 'Maybe we have to do what we came her for, then when we've done that, G–, I mean, the universe will let us go home?'

'Like what?' I rub my palms on my thighs to dry them out.

'We need to do more than simply warn Georges and Mathilde about the dangers. There's something here we've missed. We need to find out what it is and fix it, so that this world can right itself.'

'But what can we do?' Luc shrugs his shoulders. 'There is no Eiffel Tower. No way to intercept German communications. No way to win.' Luc does up the last button on his shirt.

'You come up with a better idea then,' Marianne says.

'I have.' He runs his hands through his hair, making us wait. This ought to be good. 'We go back the way we came.'

He actually said that? He said it out loud? My mouth drops open, so does Marianne's.

'You want us to go back to the battlefield?' She asks.

'Exactly.' Something ticks in Luc's jaw. It doesn't sound like he only thought of that just now.

I know I've been thinking about it, but I didn't want to say it, in case mentioning it made it real. Dizziness sets in even though I'm sitting down.

Mari stares at her brother for a while, then blinks hard.

'We arrived here during a re-enactment. We were not using real bullets and the bayonets were made of rubber. It was only pretend!'

'Going back could be suicide.' Did I say that out loud?

'Didn't say I liked it.' Luc shrugs, doing his best to look indifferent. His clenched hands betray hidden nerves. That and the trickle of sweat building on his top lip. I really should stop staring at his mouth. 'We will talk about it later. Our shift begins in an hour, we'd better get moving.' He walks out, leaving us both reeling in shock.

In nervous silence, Mari and I change into our work clothes. My long skirt slips down a little so I roll the waistband around to make it stay put.

'We are both losing weight,' Marianne says. 'My skirt is slipping too.'

'But I'm eating plenty of food. Maybe it's all the walking?'

'We are only eating two meals a day,' Marianne says. 'We eat breakfast before work, but it's really lunch, and then we eat our lunch at work, but that meal is really our dinner. Then we come home in the dark and we go to sleep.'

'Speaking of food.' I can't help rubbing my stomach. I look at the smelly sushi in the handkerchief. No thanks. 'I'll make us some biscuits.'

The only biscuits I know how to make without a recipe are called ANZACs. Grandma Heather taught me how to make them. Her mother, who would have been my great grandmother, was an Australian who went to Britain as a nurse and married an American GI after the Second World War. Grandma Heather said I had to keep the family tradition alive. We used to have fun making them and the house used to smell so good while they were in the oven.

There's no dried coconut, so I add more flour and rolled oats to compensate. Keeping busy seems like the best way to forget today's failure. It would have been so easy if it had worked. Maybe Mari is right, maybe we haven't done enough for the universe to let us go home yet.

I stir in the hot butter and golden syrup. Can't resist a taste of the uncooked dough. The sugar rush pushes down all my negative emotions. For a while at least. I can usually smell the exact time they're ready, but cooking them in the flat pan on top of the stove is more like making crunchy pancakes.

They still taste magnificent.

***

Will this shift ever end? My arms are killing me from lifting the metal templates. Marianne can't stop yawning either. The rest of the women at the tables near us are yawning too. It spreads across the factory floor like a bushfire.

Am I rude not to want to make friends? Considering our circumstances, maybe there isn't much point getting to know people. Not because they're mean or anything. I'm sure plenty of them are lovely. But what if I say the wrong thing and let slip something about history?

Worse than that, what if I start caring about them?

Which would mean I'd want to tell them what I know. Because I wouldn't want to leave my friends behind to die, would I?

The only thing I know for certain? They are so much better off not knowing what I know.

'More catchy than the flu,' Marianne hides another yawn behind her hand.

'Shake it out,' I tell her, doing a couple of quick jumps on the spot. I shake my arms out to the side and jiggle my whole body. A couple of slow, deep breaths also help.

Uh-oh, everyone is staring.

A flurry of giggles escape, but my temporary bout of silliness has worked, the yawns have stopped. 'Give it a try, shake yourselves out.'

Chuckles replace yawns as the workers get up to jiggle and wiggle. Laughter proves more infectious than yawning. I laugh so hard I snort.

'You just started a laughter club,' Marianne says, wiping her eyes.

It feels good. Damn good.

I pull the scarf off my head and tease my curls loose. I must look like a clown. It's certainly making everyone laugh. The noise we're making rivals the machinery din.

This is better than a sugar hit.

The laughs die down after a while and we're wiping our eyes and holding our tummies, sore from belly laughs. I tie my hair back into the scarf and we get back to work. I feel lighter, as if I've done something positive at last.

We keep working, but it's not such a drudge any more. The noise is my friend, blocking out those annoying stray thoughts that take me down strange laneways.

In no time at all the bell's ringing for dinner. Usually we down tools and walk out to eat, but this time the workers are all staring at me, maybe expecting another laugh? Sure, no harm in that.

I shake my hair out again and wait for the laughs. They ripple around the room. I finger comb my hair and my nails catch on a knot. 'Ow!'

It makes them laugh even harder.

Mission accomplished.

Uh-oh, Valerie walks in and everyone stops. A heavy feeling of 'I'm in trouble' kneads my belly.

Shock replaces dread. Valerie kisses both my cheeks and gives me a tight hug. 'There is so much sadness in the world. You are a spark of joy.'

Relief drains the fear away like water down a plughole. 'I thought I was in trouble!'

'You nearly were! When I first heard so much laughing, I almost walked in to tell you to shut up. But then I noticed how much extra work everyone managed afterwards. We've made nearly ten percent more uniforms today. So whatever you were laughing about, please do it again.'

***

Later than night, as we walk back to our dorm at the end of a long shift, Marianne breaks into fresh giggles. 'You should have seen your face, I thought you were going to fill your pants when Valerie walked in.'

'Me too!'

We laugh and trip over our feet as we walk home. Unfortunately, as we open the door to our room, we realize we're not alone.

Scurrying noises scrape the floorboards. The back end of a mouse disappears under a gap in the wood.

'I'm going to be sick.' I cover my mouth with my shirt.

'Let's clean up before Luc comes in and brings the mood right down.' Marianne reaches for the brush and pan and begins sweeping up a pile of black pellets on the bench top.

'Are they–?'

'–Mouse droppings.'

'Urgh!' Hugging myself does not provide a barrier to the filth of the world, but it holds me in and stops me from wigging out completely. 'The biscuits!' I've left them on the side table near my bed. Hardly a side table, more an upturned wooden fruit crate. Dammit, the lid's not on straight. I

120

move the lid and a mouse leaps out at me.

'JesusGod!'

'Calm down, it's just a mouse.'

It's no good, my whole body is tense and jerky. 'I want rat baits and I want them now.'

'Calm down. Mice are God's creatures too!'

There are teeth marks in the biscuits and black pellets too. Those things eat and poop in the same place? Gross!

'Be quiet!' Just our luck, Luc walks in. 'You sound like someone's getting killed!'

Don't tell me what to do, Luc. 'I will scream all I like. We have a rodent infestation.'

'You saw a mouse? That's what this is all about?'

'Not just a mouse. We're riddled with them. And don't look at me like that. God! You can be so patronizing! It gave me a fright, yes, but do you have any idea how many diseases mice and rats and cockroaches carry with them? My skin's crawling just thinking about it!' I scratch my arms, digging the nails in. 'First thing in the morning we buy rat pellets from the shop.'

'That's if they have them,' Luc says.

'I don't want to use poison,' Marianne says. 'If we clean up, we'll be fine. They won't come back if there's nothing here to eat.'

'I want to kill them.'

Marianne looks shocked. 'You want to kill a poor creature just because he's hungry and needs to feed his family? It is hardly the mouse's fault you left biscuits out. Now stop complaining, grab a rubbish bag and get cleaning.'

Luc shakes his head. 'Plastic bags haven't been invented yet.'

Marianne rolls her eyes. 'Fine! Then we will relight the fire in the stove and burn the rubbish instead.'

I set to wiping the benches down with soapy water and

Luc dries them with a towel. My arms ache from scrubbing hard, my hands are red raw because I keep washing them. I've never been obsessive compulsive before, but I could totally head that way. In the centre of our room, the little fire in the old stove puffs smoke every time Mari opens the door to add to the flames. The biscuits in the fire fill the room with a fresh bakery smell, then, as they burn, the air turns acrid and we have to open the windows to let it out.

'Try not to scream the dorms down,' Luc says as he heads out to the boys' area.

By the time we finish cleaning, I'm so exhausted I don't think I care about the mice any more. The bed beckons me and I crawl in. Somewhere in the walls, there are things scraping and scratching. I pull the covers up around my ears and face, leaving just a tiny opening for my nose so I can breathe.

It's impossible to turn my brain off. I'm so desperate to get home I start thinking about the logistics of the battlefield. It's the very last thing I want to do, but this nagging thought fills me with sick terror: maybe it's the only thing we can do?

'Mari, are you awake?'

'Can't sleep either huh?'

'Brain won't switch off. Do you think it would be really awful if we um . . . stayed here and kept our heads down? I mean, would that make us total cowards or would it make us smart because we were staying out of trouble?'

'I don't want to go to the front either.' Mari's voice makes it obvious she isn't the least bit close to sleep. 'I think that's why Luc's been so irritable. I bet it's all he's been thinking about, and it's too upsetting.'

It's all I've been able to think about. 'Do you think . . .'

Some kind of guilt worm crawls in my belly. 'Oh man, I just figured it out. He's known about the way back the whole time and . . .' tears choke my words away. But it all makes sense. 'Luc's known how we get back, and its so awful he'd rather live here in the uncertainty than die on the frontlines.'

'He's probably been trying to protect us.' In the darkness, I can hear Mari sniffling as well. The next moment there's a creak and the sound of feet on the floor. Mari climbs into my bed and we hug like frightened children.

Because we are frightened children.

The scritching and scratching mice noises aren't helping either.

– FIFTEEN –

THE next afternoon, the sky is gunmetal grey. Thunder rolls in from the plains. Splats of rain pelt us as we dash from the dorms to the factory door.

Avoiding one puddle, I stomp in another, splashing my legs and soaking my shoes. A visceral reminder of the day we fell through time. The same kind of storm. The same clean, metallic smell of charged particles swarming through the air.

The oncoming storm.

The rain falls harder, sounding like bullets on the factory's tin roof as we huddle under the eaves for protection. Everything reminds me of when we came here. The weather, the charged air, the tension.

Wait a second. 'Luc, Marianne, I have an idea.' If this works, we won't need to go anywhere near the war. We'll be safe at home and we can put this behind us.

Luc smiles at me. 'The thunderstorm, right?' Despite the rain, his warm expression sends ripples of something a bit weird through me. It's nice weird, not *weird* weird.

'It is pouring,' Marianne says.

It's also getting crowded as more workers arrive to start the shift. There are plenty more who are heading out, having done the early shift. They hang around the back door, waiting for a break in the rain to make a run for the dorms.

Marianne leans to my ear. 'Have umbrellas been invented?'

'This could be our chance.' Luc looks up to the darkening sky. The wind turns and drives the rain into us. Umbrellas are a moot point.

'A chance of what?' Mari asks.

'I think it was a storm that did it.' I'm thinking out loud, because the noise is driving everything out of my head anyway. It's true what they say; sometimes it is too noisy to think, like when we're inside in the factory, and the constant noise makes life easier for me. Clarity ensues, and I feel lighter all of a sudden. 'We don't have to go back to the fighting after all. We just need a storm to get us home.'

'Really?' Mari says.

A drop of rain hits my eyeball, so cold it hurts. 'We may as well give it a try.'

Luc says in his 'take charge' tone, 'Stay close, and walk out into the–'

A flash of lightning burns the air. We all jump in fright.

'–storm.'

My heart smacks into my ribs. The answering thunder shakes the ground and rattles the buildings. OK, maybe this is a bit dangerous. We haven't exactly thought it through.

But it's got to be a safer option than heading to the trenches, right?

'I think you are crazy,' Marianne says.

'What is the worst that can happen?' Luc looks to the sky again.

'We get burnt to a crisp!' Marianne says.

'Good,' he says. '*Allons-y!*'

Luc grabs my hand and pulls me into the downpour. Mari grabs hold of my other hand. For a second I'm not sure if she's pulling me back or coming with us. Confusion swirls my brain, then we're all moving off in the same direction. The three of us are out in the open. A cloudburst thumps us with such force it knocks me off balance, I trip down into the mud. If I'd fallen into a swimming pool I couldn't be any wetter.

Luc and Mari help me back to my feet, the three of us hold each other by the shoulders in a crazy stormy group hug.

Through the pelting rain comes a series of high pitched screams. The factory workers are yelling at us, beckoning us to get out of the storm.

It's all white noise and blurry vision, it's impossible to keep my eyes open in the teeming rain. Goosebumps charge along my arms. Despite the soaking, the hairs on my neck stand out. Hopeful anticipation spreads through me. A moment's discomfort ahead of our salvation? Come on, this has to work. My body is so charged I feel like we're half way home already.

Marianne yells to be heard. 'What if we get hit by lightning?'

'It will send us back home?' I shout.

'That is another movie,' Luc barks. 'But a good one at least.'

Boom! Lightning cracks the sky.

Debris flies through the air, raining pine needles and chunks of bark on us. Everything smells singed and burnt and hot-spruce-forest-y. We turn around to see a nearby pine tree smouldering. Its bark and branches are ripped away down one side, exposing bright, raw wood. Splinters and pinecones litter the ground.

I disentangle a sticky spray of pine needles from Marianne's hair.

'Zut!' Luc's shoulders slump. 'Send in the fail boat.'

I sneeze. I want to swear but my jaw clamps shut with the cold. We're still here, standing in the thumping rain. Now we'll probably get pneumonia and die.

Good one!

Henri, the foreman we met on our first day, runs out to us. The rain drowns him out as he yells something to Luc. Luc shakes his head and wipes the rain from his face. Which is utterly pointless because as he wipes it clear, fresh rain splatters his face.

Why has Henri come out here? He's shouting something but I can't make it out. He clamps his hand around Mari's arm and drags her. Mari is holding me, so I get pulled along. Oh, I'm still holding on to Luc, so he's coming too.

We reach the safety of the factory eaves. We're utterly drenched but at least the rain isn't pelting us in the face any more so we can see better.

'You could have been killed!' Henri has a wild and crazy look about him. Has he always been this tall? I thought he was more hunched. And that look on his face is not at all his usual dopey expression. I'm doubly confused because he looks so familiar again. Is he from Amiens perhaps? This is sending me mad.

And hey, he's speaking perfect English. Unless the lightning hit me in the head and I can understand French?

No, everyone else is babbling in French. Henri is speaking in English. From everyone else's tone, I think they're saying we were mad to be out in the rain.

We create puddles on the factory floor with each step. 'Everyone is delighted you are unharmed,' Henri says as he marches Mari and I to the change rooms. 'But you have also made a mess of puddles that you will have to clean up.

In the women's change room are fresh, dry uniforms for us to wear.

'Thank you,' Marianne says. She has to raise her voice over the noise of rain on the tin roof.

Henri looks as if he's about to say something, then that slow, almost sly look comes over his face and those dead eyes are back. His posture has slumped since we came inside.

'I would not have picked Henri to come to our rescue,' Marianne says as she wrings out her wet hair into the sink.

The cold has well and truly kicked in. The wet uniform is five times heavier than normal and takes serious effort to get off. There's no towel in here, so I pull dry clothes over my goose bumps and put up with the shivering.

'You know something? I don't think Henri is all that slow, I think he's pretending.' The woollen socks stick to my legs as I pull them on. 'He was speaking English to us, you know? I thought he was so dumb he barely spoke French. And seriously, does he remind you of anyone, because it's bugging me something chronic.'

'Why would he pretend to be disabled?'

'Because just like Luc, he's the right age to be sent off to war isn't he? He's fit and healthy, but y'know, he presents as a bit gone in the head so he doesn't have to go and fight.'

'That is extreme.'

'Better than being dead.' I sneeze again. My fingers tremble against the shirt buttons.

'Are you still cold?' Marianne's wet hair hangs limply around her face.

'Frozen to the marrow.' I breathe on my hands to warm them up.

Mari helps button me up.

'Thanks.'

We earn stares from the staff when we get to our workbench.

Word must have spread about us standing out in the thunderstorm. In hindsight it was a spectacularly dopey thing to do, but it also could have worked. If we hadn't done anything, we'd be kicking ourselves for the missed opportunity.

But how to explain what the heck we were doing out there? Probably safer to just ignore everyone and get stuck in to work.

The chalk wafer keeps spilling from my frozen fingers, but the bonus with being wet, a little damp hair soon erases my mistakes and I keep right on working. I'm not sure if I've thawed out or become used to the cold. At least I'm not working with cold water like Luc, out in the wash troughs with the woollen fabric.

Eventually it's time for a break. I want to sneak out to see how Luc is doing, check whether he's frozen to death. But the women here look at me expectantly. They want some laughter club. OK, I'll give it to them, even if my heart's not in it. I thought we had a chance to go home. I was wrong. Life is dishing out one disappointment after the other.

But what do you know? Even fake laughter leads to the real thing, and we're cracking up for real.

Maybe I'm cracked too?

***

At dinner, the hot food should be helping my mood and it's thawing out my core temperature. But I'm still flailing in my head about why the storm didn't send us back. The conditions were so similar. 'Has aspirin been invented yet?'

'I can ask Valerie for something medical.' Marianne looks about the room for our supervisor.

Luc picks up his fork and digs in. 'I saw her out the back, she was yelling at Henri.'

Oh really? 'What about?'

Luc shovels in more hot food, then says, 'I couldn't make it out over my chattering teeth.'

'Maybe she didn't want him to catch his death of cold?' Marianne says between slurps of soup.

The soup bowl serves a dual purpose of warming my fingers, so I hold it and slurp it from the side, like the convicts must have done back in eighteen whenever.

The meal has helped my mood, but it hasn't solved all my issues by a long shot. 'I really need something for this headache I'm starting to get.'

'Come on, let's find Valerie,' Mari stands up and takes my hand.

Leaving the mess hall early, it's strange to not hear the comforting machinery sounds as we head towards Valerie's office.

She has her back to us and she's lecturing Henri about something because her hands are waving about.

A few steps closer to the office, Henry's face comes into view. He looks like a puppy about to get his nose rubbed in it. A flicker of recognition crosses his face, then he drops back to looking glum. It's driving me insane that I can't place him.

Valerie spins around and sees us. I wanted to find her, but now that I have I want to run away.

'What do you want?'

'I'm sorry, but I have a massive headache and I need something for it. I thought you might have something.'

Hands on hips, Valerie says, 'Do I look like a drug dealer to you?'

Whoa, overreaction much? 'I need an aspirin.' Now I feel sick in the stomach as well.

Marianne steps up. 'We also wanted to thank Henri for saving us. My brother . . . was trying to conduct a crazy experiment . . . if not for Henri we might have been struck by lightning. He was very brave.'

'He was very stupid!' Valerie says. 'And so were the three of you! Standing there in the middle of a storm. Henri, make Ingrid some poppy tea. And don't you dare have any yourself, you great oaf!'

Does she have to lay the stupid on so thick? Wait a minute, just as Henri turns, I swear he looks like one of the soldiers in the trenches that day. Did he come back with us? Is that why he's playing so dumb? He's a fit and healthy adult who, like us, is doing whatever he can to stay away from the frontlines. Maybe he slipped back with a different group? Maybe heaps more people fell through time that day.

Valerie tilts her head to the side, making it click. 'Marianne, you should get back to work. Ingrid, as soon as you've had your drink, you can join them.'

Suddenly I'm alone with Henri in Valerie's office. He turns his back on me and switches on a kettle. Holy cow, it's electric! I don't know if they belong in this time or not, but after the Eiffel Tower fiasco, I wouldn't be surprised to see a laptop laying about. Who knows what they have in this world.

Henri potters about for a bit, then hands me a mug of warm liquid. Here's a trust exercise if ever there was one.

I take a sip, the headache thumps on. 'How long till it starts working?'

Henri's eyes flicker and he gives a sly grin. His words sound slow and deliberate. 'You a pretty girl.'

In English, for my benefit, but heavily accented. For a second I weight up the pros and cons of questioning him, wondering if he'll tell me the truth or become super angry. In the end, curiosity has me in its grip and I have to ask, 'Why did you run out into the rain to save us? You could have caught pneumonia or been struck by lightning.'

His dopey grin stays in place.

'Were you there in the trenches with us? Were you part of the cosplay? Is that why you're here?'

Right there in front of me, something dies in his eyes. He must have been playing this part for a long time. Sipping more tea, my tongue and lips turn fuzzy. It's numbing the back of my throat, but my headache keeps thumping away. 'What's in this stuff?'

Another slurred grin. I silently count to five before he says, 'Poppy.'

'Yeah, Valerie called it that. Is that the brand or something? Like Earl Grey?'

Another five seconds, yet another dopey grin. 'Poppy. Pretty flower. Like pretty girl.'

'Ri-i-i-i-ight.' My headache is strong and true, while my tongue has grown to twice its normal size. I'll end up like Henri soon.

Maybe poppy tea is his secret?

He keeps looking at me with that leery grin. Come on mate, you were lucid when you grabbed us out of the rain. 'I know you're faking it. You don't want to go to war. I don't blame you. I don't want you to go to war either. I won't tell anyone. Your secret is safe with me.'

Those dead eyes flicker for a second, as if something penetrates his thoughts. He draws a slow circle on the leg of his pants with his finger.

'Are we're just going to stare at each other and pretend you're soft in the head and I'm stupid?'

Henri belches and laughs like an idiot.

'I can see right through you. You know my secret, I'm a

hundred years out of time. And this isn't even our world. That's your secret too, so why don't you own it?'

A sway of his head, his eyes make slow blinks, then when he opens them they are hard and sharp. 'Don't make me the enemy. Not when I am the only one who can help you.'

Chills streak down my neck and some of the poppy tea comes back up. This guy is seriously freaking me out.

***

Back at my workstation, I tell Mari every little thing I learned about Henri. We don't have to keep our voices low, the machinery is like a cone of silence over us, blocking eavesdroppers.

'I can see why it would do him no good to come clean,' Mari says. 'He'd only be dragged off to the frontlines.'

'I'm not saying he should let *everyone* know. I'm just saying that I know, and now you know. Y'know?' My headache hasn't budged but I feel warmer inside. And a bit drowsy. Thanks a lot, poppy tea.

Mari says, 'I think we should drop it.'

I'm not going to. 'He might know how to get us home. He said he could help us.'

'Really?'

'Um, I mean, he said something like he was the only one who could help us.'

Mari creases her brows. 'He is not helping very much. I think you're right. I think we have met him before, but I simply cannot remember when. Some days it's on the tip of my tongue, and then, like a snowflake, it melts away.'

'That's really beautiful, Mari.'

'I've been reading poetry. Valerie let me borrow a book she enjoys.'

'Valerie. She's confusing too. She's tough but I think under all that she cares a bit. I mean, clearly she's looking after Henri as well. Don't worry, I'm not going to expose him, if that's what you're worried about.'

'Good.' She chews her lower lip with worry. 'Because if the army comes here to take Henri away, they will take Luc too.'

'But he's only sixteen. Doesn't he have to be eighteen or something?'

'In our world maybe, but who knows what the rules are here? And compared to everyone else, he's so tall he looks like he's twenty.'

'Oh God, you're right. We are so screwed.'

– SIXTEEN –

BACK home, or back *when*, I'd normally sleep in on Sundays. Saturdays too. And Thursday mornings because I had a first session free so I didn't have to turn up to school until nine forty-seven.

No such chance of a lazy start today, Mari is shoving my shoulder, saying something about church. Is she serious?

I bet Luc's sleeping in, over in the boys' dorm. I bet she doesn't try and drag him off to church.

Can I smell chocolate? I flick the sleep from my eyes and see Luc walking in, with a plate of chocolate croissants and a newspaper under his arm. Pinch me, I'm dreaming. When he's not being bossy, Luc can be quite considerate. It's enough to get me out of bed at any rate. Would you look at that? I slept in my clothes again. Ah well, saves time getting dressed in the morning.

'I did not think shops were open on Sunday?' Marianne says.

'The bakery is essential to the war effort . . . or something.'

Sundays are more like Wednesdays, because they're in the middle of our working week. We'll be working this afternoon as usual. So why are we up so early? I grab a croissant, say thanks and climb back into bed.

Rain is tripping on the roof, growing heavier. I thought we were moving into Summer but maybe the seasons are all arse-about in this world.

Despite the bed-bugs and the no food in the dorm rule, I'm warm again under the covers, eating my buttery chocolately breakfast. In the last few days, we've collected wood in the rain, from the shards of the exploded pine tree. The wood now sizzles as it burns in our little stove, filling the room with smoky, spruce forest smells.

'What news of the war?' Mari asks.

That's the kind of thing to make me want to pay attention. I pretend I'm not, but can't help it. I chew quietly so I can listen. I can't get my news any other way, because there's no internet or television. There was a radio back at the Gaillard's house, but I haven't heard one since we started worked at the factory.

=...' he turns the page. 'Oh dear. Someone has told them about Henri putting his life on the line to rescue three *waifs* caught in a storm.'

Marianne groans, 'Oh no.'

I sit up in bed and brush the crumbs away. Luc has my full attention as he translates the report.

'The gentle giant, who was perhaps too simple to understand the dangers of the situation, risked his life to bring the three factory workers out of harm's way.

'Such was the ferocity of the storm, lightning struck a nearby cedar and cleaved it in two. The children were apparently frozen witless in the rain, so shocked they were unable to move. Witnesses say Monsieur Henri Ederle ran out to the three terrified children and led them to safety. His actions are representative of the elan *shared by all*

good Frenchmen, to protect and keep safe all sons and daughters of France.'

'That's so patronizing.' It's not at all what happened and we know it.

Luc closes the newspaper.

I sit up and shake the crumbs out of bed, then head over to sit by the fire to keep warm. 'He's only playing dumb. Trying to hide in plain sight. He was there in the trenches with us, back in our time. I'm sure of it.' That earns me a nod from Luc. Some kind of bond is developing between us, the three of us I mean. Not just me and Luc, but me, Luc and Mari. We're in this together, we're getting out of it together. Bonding is so much better than fighting and bickering. And much, much nicer than Luc pretending to be in charge and making all the decisions. I'm making decisions too. It's kind of nice, but it's a responsibility I'd be glad to chuck as soon as we're home. Making decisions for other people sucks!

'We need to be careful.' Marianne shakes her head. 'If Henri gets too much attention, they will notice you too, Luc.'

Silence for a while as we digest this. If we all believe Henri was in the trenches that day with us, does he recognise us? Maybe my orange hair has given the three of us away?

'It's not helping that we're in the papers, but it's not a huge story,' I speak more in hope than anything else. 'It'll blow over, won't it?'

Luc puts the folded paper on the shelf and says, 'Yeah, of course it will.' His worried expression doesn't match his flippant tone.

'Oh, I just remembered. I wonder if my recipe made it in? Mari turned it into French for me.'

Luc gives me with raised brow. Am I in trouble?

'There was a notice up in the lunchroom,' I explain. 'It was calling on people to offer recipes for victory. To help feed the troops. So I wrote out the recipe for ANZAC biscuits. Why are you looking at me like that?'

'Because we're trying not to get noticed!' Luc says.

All those nice feelings I have for Luc evaporate. 'Sorry for trying to help!' Hot anger surges inside me. 'It's not like they don't have them already. The Australian troops will be sharing them around when they get here anyway. Or maybe they're here already. I'm not sure. Anyway, I didn't call them ANZACs, I called them Victory Biscuits.'

Mari nods. 'We need to be doing something to help. Surely that is why we were brought here, so we can make a difference? Maybe only in a small way but every little bit helps.'

'Thank you Mari.' An invisible weight slides off my shoulders. 'Anyway, it's only biscuits. It's not like it will make a massive difference to the outcome.'

Mari shrugs and turns to Luc. 'What did they have to eat, the soldiers?'

'Army rations, but I don't know exactly what. And I don't know if it's the same in this world anyway. What is in your Victory biscuits?'

'Um . . . Oats, flour, sugar, golden syrup and butter. Dried coconut if you can get it. But who knows, maybe in this world coconut hasn't been invented. By the way, I haven't made any biscuits in here since the mice ate the last lot. I don't think they've come back.'

'No milk?' Luc asks as he flicks through the paper. 'Here it is. They printed it.'

'Yay, I'm published!' I have to take my wins where I can. 'Um, no, there's no milk so they stay fresh enough to last the trip from Australia to Europe on a ship without going mouldy.'

Suddenly Luc jumps up, grabs me by the shoulders and kisses both my cheeks, sending lightning bolts of shock through me. 'You are a genius!'

Confusion doesn't even come close to describing how I feel. A second ago he was ticking me off, now he's kissing me. Talk about emotional whiplash. I manage to croak, 'thanks.'

'Maybe this is the difference we are here to make?' Marianne says. 'Just a small difference, but an important one. 'An army marches on its stomach' and all that.'

'Maybe.' Luc keeps smiling at me and something flips low in my belly. 'All that sugar and syrup would give them energy too. Hang on, how did you get hold of sugar?'

'Um, it was in the shop.'

Luc scratches the back of his neck. 'Sugar is supposed to be in short supply. Just when I think I have this world figured out, it messes me up again. Same goes for the golden syrup. I wouldn't have thought you could get that.'

'It was really cheap.' I show Luc the jar of syrup, complete with the Canadian flag. 'In our case I used maple syrup instead because they didn't have golden syrup, but it's pretty much the same.'

'This must mean the Canadians are here. God bless them,' Mari says.

In the distance, the town's church bells ring. So shoot me, I can't help think they sound like a wedding. I must be so tired and worn down to even think like that. That's what it is. I'm exhausted and ready to cry at any moment. Just like the contestants on *Home Fixers*, who start crying by the second episode.

I have to remind myself that it's the stress of the situation we're in. I'm not my usual self. I've been off my meds for how long now? And as for Luc, my reaction to him is probably no more than him being the only boy around, and he can be nice. At times. That must be why my emotions are racing off without my brain.

Marianne's face fills with light. 'I believe Ingrid's recipe could be our contribution to this world. When they start feeding them to the troops, it could make all the difference. Now, let us go to church.'

The what now?

***

It's eight thirty when we climb the stone steps to the church's heavy timber doors. The doors are flung open and people are filing in. Marianne stops so suddenly, I crash into the back of her. She dips her finger into a granite bowl set into the wall, then touches her head, chest and both shoulders. Luc does the same. I copy them so I don't stand out as clueless.

I follow them towards a bench seat. Luc leans towards me and whispers, 'We haven't got a prayer.'

I can't help giggling. That kind of flippancy will send me straight to hell.

'Stop it you two, we are in a house of God.'

Thanks for the reminder Mari.

Standing here in the aisle, Marianne drops to one knee before taking a seat. Luc does the same so I copy again. How do people know how to do all these things?

Luc leans in again, 'Mari thinks we can pray ourselves home.'

Mari hisses back, 'It's a lot safer than waiting for a bolt of lighting.'

Bolts of lightning. Oh dear. What if The Big Man zaps

me for being an imposter in His house? On the other hand, we stood in a thunderstorm with lightning whizzing around us. He had every chance to smack us down and He didn't take it.

There are more people here than were out in the rain, maybe He is waiting for a bigger audience, to make an example of us?

Time to pray for this nagging anxiety to go away. That feeling of not being in control could so easily take over.

And whose to say prayer won't work? Mari's so religious; her prayers should cover us as well, right? We're in this together and all that.

I pray a bit harder, just to be on the safe side.

Something shifts inside me, as if guilt is real and physical. Uh-oh, does God know something I don't? Does He know I'm not being serious about this? Because I totally am. Seriously, God, if you can hear me, I've learned my lesson and I'll be good and go to church every week when I get home. If you could just see to it that I get home, OK?

'What do we do now, sister?' Luc asks Mari.

'We keep praying.' Mari flattens her hands together and kneels on the timber plank below us.

That's good, because I started praying almost before I sat down.

'Do we all pray the same thing?' Luc asks. 'Or is this a free session?'

Marianne keeps her head down. 'We pray for our deliverance.'

Luc bows his head. I do too, trying very hard to switch off the running commentary in my head. The one telling me it won't work. The one complaining about how my knees hurt. The one noticing the smell of incense and wet cardigans around me as more people shuffle in and take their seats.

'Please, God, I'm sorry for whatever I did.' Because I

must have done something really horrible to end up here. Maybe I've been selfish or something? In which case, 'God, you don't have to answer my prayers. Just answer Mari's instead. She has loads better faith than me.'

Then it hits me, like a smack inside my head and maybe God is teaching me a lesson or something. I have been selfish. I haven't been as nice as I should have been to Luc and Mari, I've argued and bitched and moaned about everything.

And there's a war on, and all I've been thinking about is running away. When did I actually think about helping other people? A biscuit recipe doesn't count, not really. I need to be a better person.

But I barely know where to start.

Two boys, wearing long white cloaks, walk down the aisles and open more doors for the crowds to come in.

A cold draught flies under my skirt and tickles the back of my legs. It's so cold in here. I guess it's too much to pray for central heating?

More people walk in, all doing the quick kneel and bob before taking a seat. It gets crowded pretty quickly.

Luc says, 'There will be another service after this, at eleven thirty. Look at the notice board over there.' He nods in the direction of a timber frame on the wall, with its ornate rows of block letters and times.

'Three services in one day? Wow, I guess people pray more when there's a war on, huh?'

'I guess they do.' He gives me the most disarming smile, making me feel funny inside. Am I so starved of attention that this is all it takes? Luc is probably praying to be a nicer person too, that must be what's going on. So he's starting now, being nicer to me?

I can be nice.

I think.

Marianne glares at us. 'Can you two stop flirting and get back to praying? It will not work if it is just me, we need to focus our prayers on our return home.'

We weren't flirting. Well, I'm pretty sure I wasn't. Why would Mari think I'm flirting when I'm just being nice? I wish I could switch that voice off in my head. Please God, get me home so I can get my tablets.

Time to put all my mental effort into the prayer. Eyes shut tight, I concentrate on the most positive thoughts and very best intentions, with promises to be good thrown in. I'm making a bargain with God.

Then a sick thought creeps in and I can't stop it. If a bargain with God doesn't work, will I end up making a deal with the devil instead?

Dammit! Every time I open my eyes, we are still in the church.

Oops, better not cuss in here. *Shut the front door*! There, that's better.

Pain shoots into my knees from the kneeling. No use fighting it, I would prefer this pain for a short while as opposed to the alternative of being stuck in this world forever.

Sounds of footsteps nearby mean more people are filing in. Closing in on us. 'Mari?' I lean over. 'If this doesn't work, we'll have to move out, they'll be starting the next service soon.'

Marianne shakes her head. 'We are not going anywhere until we receive God's blessing.'

Archaeologists will find us one day, three skeletons praying on the bench. 'Are we staying?' I murmur to Luc.

'It seems that way.'

'But.' I drop my voice to a murmur. 'I'm not Catholic. What if they kick me out?'

'They won't kick you out.' Luc squeezes my hand and

it's impressive how reassured I feel. 'Just follow my lead and you will be fine. It will all be over in an hour or so.'

An hour? OK God, you've got me for an hour. I can sleep when we get home.

The service begins. I follow Luc's lead so that I know when to stand, when to kneel, when to sit. Every time we sit, I twirl my ankles to get the blood circulating into my feet again. The last time I went to church was for my cousin's wedding. That had been a little timber chapel at a vineyard, filled with flowers and ribbons. Probably not even a real church, just a building that looked like one. It was nothing compared to this grand stone behemoth with its cavernous, criss-cross ceiling and stained glass windows. And so many statues of tortured saints.

Incense smoke swirls through the air. It should make me cough, but I end up liking it. The smell reminds me of fresh soap and scented candles. Light shines through the glass mosaic windows, catching on the smoke. Magical fingers of light touch all the people inside. Serenity cloaks me, even though I don't have a clue what the priest is saying.

'He is speaking in Latin,' Luc whispers.

'Oh.' What's one more language eh? Maybe in this world, everyone speaks five languages. That would be cool.

I catch sight of Mari. She has a wistful look on her face, as if all that kneeling, praying, kneeling, sitting and kneeling again gives her joy. It probably does. If I can get in the right headspace, I'll start enjoying it too.

Whoa, now we're standing up and I have to breathe a little harder because I stood up too fast and got lightheaded.

People are making their way to the aisles and walking down to the front. I stand to follow but Mari turns and puts a hand on my shoulder, making me sit back. 'Only confirmed Catholics can receive the sacrament, you need to stay here.'

For a second I mishear her and wonder what the sack-of-mints are. Then it clicks. 'Oh.'

Out of the whole congregation, only myself and a few children, aged about five or six, stay in their seats. I've never felt so self-conscious.

I keep my head down and look about for something to pass the time. Oh well, could always flip open the spare bible. After pretending to read, I look up to check on how Luc and Marianne are progressing. The bottom drops out of my stomach as I see two familiar faces. Valerie and Henri.

Henri is giving his best zonked-out expression, as per usual, while Valerie looks full of purpose and energy. She sees me and gives an imperious nod. This is a whole world of wrong. Those two are up to something, I just know it. But the two of them know I wouldn't dare make a scene here in a church, so I have to sit here and watch them, saying nothing.

Slowly, Marianne and Luc nudge forward until it's their turn to receive the sacrament. They open their mouths and accept the wafer, then mutter something to the priest. Then they move to the side and take a sip from this golden goblet. It's all very mystical and I kind of wish I was Catholic so I could join in. I wonder what I have to do to be one?

Soon enough it's Valerie and Henri's turn for the wafer and wine. As they begin to walk back, a beam of light shines across the pews.

Henri walks through the beam, cries out and falls to the ground.

Wait—what?

Strangled noises escape from Henri, as if something

hideous is leaving his body. And to think, I was doing my best to behave myself and not make a scene, but Henri's absolutely going for it.

Everyone is staring at him and gasping. Oh come on, overplaying it much?

Marianne and Luc rush over to see what's going on. I stand on our bench seat to get a better look.

'*Merci, jezhyu!*' Henri's voice–so clear and confident I barely recognize it–carries through the church. At first I think he's sneezing, then I realise he's thanking Jesus. I think.

'*Son un miracla!*' Valerie's turn now. What's 'mi-rah-cla'? Oh wait, *miracle.*

Mayhem breaks out as people swoon and gasp and fall to their knees in prayer crying out in French and probably a bit of Latin and a few bits of English. The priest loses his place; he's too distracted to keep going. He quickly hands his goblet over to a young boy and dashes towards the chaos.

'Give this soul room to breathe,' the priest says. Ah, now he's speaking English.

Bonkers!

Henri cries out this big long tirade of stuff that I don't get at all.

Luc reaches me and translates, so I'm not completely out of the loop. 'He is saying he's prayed to Saint Denis for years. He says he's an adult trapped inside a child's mind.'

Sounds like a total crock to me.

People cry out and start crossing themselves, some swoon and wail. Then suddenly people are pointing to us and Luc quickly translates again. 'He saved the children of the storm.'

Children of the storm? Oh please!

Shame washes over me, I'm hot and cold and fuzzy all at once. Maybe this is a miracle and instead of praying and hoping for some of it to rub off on me, I've disrespected God and now I'll never get home.

Oh God I'm so confused!

People push and shove to get closer to Henri the 'miracle man'. Hands reach through the air as they grope his head, body, clothes and feet.

So many of the factory workers are in the church this morning. They know all about the time we stood in the thunderstorm. If they didn't see it for themselves, they told each other or read it in the newspaper as well.

Henri's transformation feels wrong. It's all too convenient, isn't it? Henri played dumb, I called his bluff, and now he's completely normal. No Henri, you're the one disrespecting God with this fake show. Not that anyone else has worked it out. The crowd is in raptures about the spectacle in the church.

God, they're so gullible.

I desperately try not to fidget. I want out of here and I want out now. The priests up the front clear their throats and press on with the rest of the service. Has it been an hour? Has it been two? Henri's show must have added at lest twenty minutes at any rate.

Finally, we can go. People want to stop and talk about Henri's miracle while I want to scream. Mari has more patience with them and stays behind to chat.

'Come on, Mari! We have to get ready for work.' Luc sounds way more reasonable than I could be right now.

He manages to drag her away and we're free of the madness.

'They are worn down by four years of war. They need miracles. This has done them the world of good. Given them something positive to talk about,' Marianne says as we walk back to our dorm.

Quick check behind me to make sure no one else can hear me. 'He's a big fat fake! If he's cured of . . . of . . . whatever he was pretending he had, then I'm the Queen of England.'

'Do not speak blasphemy!' Mari says. 'We all saw it happen. Right before our eyes.'

'But we know he was pretending to be crazy all along, to get out of war service.'

Mari shakes her head. 'If that truly was the case, why would he choose a church, in such public view, to fake his miracle recovery? Knowing he'd have the wrath of God on him for lying?'

Ever since we fell through time, I haven't had any answers, and I sure don't have an answer to this one either. I'm so frustrated and crazy and angry with this world.

I'm also getting so desperate I'm willing to face the frontline, just to get this over with.

I've had enough.

Enough!

– SEVENTEEN –

WE GET an answer of sorts at work. No sign of Henri, which surprises me. What's the point of making a big show about his transformation if he goes into hiding?

Valerie calls all our attention at dinner break. 'Henri is following his calling to serve God in whichever way He sees fit. Henri will no longer be working here as he is entering the priesthood.'

OK, so that's why.

For the next few minutes, none of what Valerie says rings true, but I can't interrupt her or anything, obviously, otherwise everyone will turn on me. As far as they're concerned, Henri is a hero and has now been chosen by God.

'If anyone would like to put their name forward for the position of foreman, please let me know,' Valerie says, then ads, 'thank you everyone, and enjoy your meals.'

'I always thought it would be so romantic to be a nun,' Mari says as we finish the last few bites.

Luc and I lock gazes and burst out laughing.

'You can't be serious?' he says.

'Yes I can. And why do you always put down the things I feel passionate about?' Mari puts her knife and fork together with a clatter.

Well, OK. We should be kinder to each other. We're all under strain and we need to watch out for that. We can't get home if we're pulling in different directions.

'Henri following God is too convenient,' Luc says.

'That's exactly what I was thinking!'

'I doubt in this world they are putting priests on the front line,' Luc says. 'I bet you anything he starts questioning his faith right about the time armistice is declared.'

I nod in agreement and play with my food.

Mari says, 'I think it's noble.'

Luc shrugs and drinks the last of his water.

It's a smart move though, to get away from the heat of battle. What do we have? Nothing. Sure, we want to go home, but it's like a beggar wanting to be a millionaire. It's all well and good to dream, but we don't know how to get there. We've tried hypnosis, standing in storms and then prayer and we're still here.

We can't keep ignoring the elephant in the room. Maybe the only way home is to go back the way we came. But how exactly do we do that without getting killed?

'Shame only Henri got a miracle. I could use a few right now.' Is it selfish of me to want a miracle?

Marianne sighs. 'Perhaps we have not done what we came here for.'

I'm about to ridicule Marianne for once again claiming some higher power is at work. But my words catch in my throat. A queasy, scared feeling spreads through me. Maybe we haven't done what we came here for after all. We sit here, looking at each other. All the time I can't work out how three high school students are going to make a jot of difference to a world gone mad.

Luc covers my hand with his, his face kind and sympathetic. As usual I'm reading way too much into it. 'I suppose it was too much to ask that a simple biscuit recipe could save the world,' he says.

A bell chimes, the meal is over, time to tuck my hair into the scarf and get back to work.

***

I'm on auto-pilot as I roll out the cloth, slap down the template and trace the chalky wedge around the edge. A sob catches in my throat. The line on the fabric looks exactly like police outlines on pavements. The ones they draw to show where a victim died.

Another dead body.

I can't let go of the template and draw the next outline. My brain shuts down. The metal plate is glued to my hands, my heart hammering as loud as cannon fire.

'Ingrid? Answer me.' Mari, taps my shoulder.

'I think I'm getting depression,' As soon as the words are out, I feel their truth. 'I can't do this any more.'

'Come here.' Marianne gives me a hug. 'We will tell Valerie you have a headache and you can go and lie down.'

A lie down? Maybe in a deep, dark cave and not wake up until all this is over. But it's never going to be over, is it? We are stuck, one hundred years in the past, in the wrong universe, no way of knowing how this ends and no way of getting home.

'We will get through this. I know we will.' Mari says. It's amazing how confident people can sound even when you know they're talking rubbish.

Mari helps me roll out more fabric and puts the template over it, ready to trace another outline. Another dead man on the ground.

Luc rushes in to the cutting room, his face pastier than the chalk in my hands. 'Girls, we have a problem. Look at

151

this.' He shows us a bolt of red fabric.

'That is not blue.' Have I've mentioned before how good I am at stating the obvious?

Luc gulps. 'They're using this for the kepi, the red caps for the officers. But it's also for trousers. For everyone!'

So far all we've done is draw outlines for jackets and long coats, trousers will make a change from the routine. But red? My eyes peel open in shock 'Talk about make them a target.'

'Keep your voice down,' Luc says.

'Attention everyone.' Valerie walks in to the workroom. Everyone downs tools to listen to her speech, which Mari dutifully translates for me. 'We are changing procedures today and will be cutting trouser patterns for the rest of the month. Everybody needs to collect a template from the storeroom. Be careful, these metal templates are new and could have sharp edges.'

Sick dread burns the back of my throat. Why would any sane country dress her soldiers in pants the colour of blood?

Luc leans closer to me. So close his breath tickles my ear. 'In our world, they got rid of the red trousers in nineteen fourteen, right at the start of the war, because the troops were too easy to see. It's the machine guns, you see, you can kill dozens of people from a long way off. Red is suicide.'

I try and remember back to the time the soldiers rescued me from the real gunfire. I was too busy freaking out about live ammunition to pay much attention to clothes. From memory, everyone was coated in mud.

Maybe that's how they disguised the colour? By muddying up, they had a better chance at camouflage than being in bright red. I grab the edge of the table to steady myself. Luc's voice croaks as he turns to Valerie, his hands gesticulating near the fabric as he speaks in rapid French, in what I can only imagine is his attempt to argue they cannot use red fabric to make trousers.

Valerie stares daggers at him.

Uh oh.

There is a lot of blather after that, back and forth, but I get the gist of it. Valerie is giving Luc a right ticking off.

The room turns deathly quiet as all the workers stop pushing the fabric through their sewing machines to watch the exchange.

Mari murmurs in my ear, 'Luc is saying this war is different. That in battles past, the sight of thousands in a bright uniform, marching towards a battlefield, struck fear into the hearts of the enemy. But this is a new war, and the machine guns can reach further. The soldiers do not stand a chance.'

'*Seelons!*' Valerie turns a shade of red, just like the fabric, but Luc isn't going quietly.

'The *Boche* have machine guns,' he's shouting now, 'the guns cover incredible distances. Soldiers in red pants become walking targets. Their entire uniforms should be made to blend in, not stand out.'

Valerie's voice takes on a steely edge and she spits as she speaks.

Mari's voice drops even lower, 'She is accusing Luc of knowing better than the French Army.'

Luc's Adam's apple bobs sharply. All of a sudden I notice how lean and defined his neck has become. I have an inappropriate urge to kiss him right where the curve meets his shoulder. Jesus, what is *wrong* with me? This is going badly and all I can do is ogle Luc's neck?

Valerie keeps menacing Luc in French and all I can see are dead soldiers in these bright red pants. I have to stand up to Valerie.

I have to step up. 'Translate for me, would you Mari?' I clear my throat and say loud and clear, 'Do not attack

Luc. He is protecting me.'

Like a crowd at a tennis match, all eyes swing to me. Public speaking? I'd better nail this. 'He is protecting my vision. I have been praying to God, and He answered my prayers.'

Mari keeps translating, when she stops, I figure it's my turn to speak again. 'You too have witnessed His blessings on Henri. That same day God cured Henri, I had a vision. A sign that God is on our side.'

Valerie blinks and shifts her weight. 'A vision, you say?' She speaks to me in English.

'Well, I mean, not so much a vision. More a voice. I prayed to God to help us find a way to defeat our enemies.' My heart hammers in my chest as I wait for Mari to translate, then I'm all-in. 'He told me we must make the whole uniform the same pale blue colour, to protect our soldiers so they cannot be seen and then killed from far away. No more red trousers. He also said we must build a radio receiving tower, tall enough so we can hear what the enemy are saying. We need to build another Eiffel Tower.'

Some of the women drop to their knees and noisily pray. Valerie stands, open mouthed, staring at me. No way can she dispute my vision, because doing that would raise questions about Henri's miracle. And the people around here seem pretty fond of miracles.

Taut silence stretches between us, until Valerie blinks and says, 'I see.'

I exhale at last. My knees are shaking.

Valerie steps towards her office, then turns back, as if having second thoughts. 'In light of this blessing from the Almighty, I will send a telegram to army headquarters and tell them of your conversation with God.'

Marianne groans and drops to the floor. I rush to her side and give her that hug we both need. Luc is helping her up, saying things like 'well done' and 'brilliant' to the two of us.

Mari looks at me with a tear-stained face. 'May God forgive us for what we have done.'

Luc's face is full of admiration, and it's directed right at me. 'If the army does what you say, it could turn this whole thing around.'

More workers crowd around us, touching us on the shoulders and head.

Luc embraces us in a three-way squish. 'You did the right thing. God is on our side. This horrible war will be over soon.'

Warmth and light chase away the splinters of fear inside me. Maybe this is the reason we came, and the universe will let us go home soon?

***

Turns out, we still have to use the red material, but only to make kepis. Because Valerie tells us the Army will not allow the fabric to go to waste. We could make doona covers out of it instead.

I think back to that tall officer in the re-enactment, the one wearing the red cap. I can't remember his face, it was so long ago and I wasn't paying attention. Story of my life. I just hope whoever ends up wearing these bright red hats slathers them in mud first.

It's still raining and I'm in a foul mood because, as Mathilde Gaillard once said, 'the English have arrived'. It probably should have happened a couple of weeks ago, but with all the stress and shock, it took its time turning up. How strange to be grateful I'm in nineteen sixteenish, with the pad machine in the ladies' toilets. If we were in proper history I'd probably have to wear rags.

Luc carries three bolts of pale blue fabric in his arms as

he walks in to the pattern marking area. Valerie walks directly behind him, carrying nothing.

'Attention!' Her voice carries clear across the room.

Mari steps in close to translate for me as Valerie addresses the factory in French.

'The army has decreed to change the trousers to horizon blue. You will . . . retrieve a template and get to work right away. Because of the delays, we must make up time. You will all be . . . required to work two extra hours per shift.'

Luc dumps the blue fabric down on the table. He hugs me by surprise, then kisses both cheeks. 'You did it!'

'You may have God on your side, but those trousers will not make themselves,' Valerie says in her lilting English. 'Less chat, more work.'

'Thank you, Valerie.' I feel a surge of gratitude. 'Thank you for listening.'

Valerie steps towards me and I wish I'd shut my mouth. 'I passed on a message, that is all. But know this. If one extra countryman dies because of your vision, his blood will be on your hands.' She turns and walks back to the delivery bay, the queen of the dramatic exit.

'Come on, let's do as she says.' Working might loosen the guilt sticking to my ribs.

'Do you think we have done what we came for?' Mari asks Luc.

'I hope so.' Scratching the back of his neck.

'Then . . . maybe we should try to go home again?' Mari's eyes shine with hope.

'No argument with me. What about you Ingrid?'

'Yes, I really want to go home too.'

Mari says, 'Good. Now we simply need to find a way to do it.'

It's time to say this out loud and deal with it. 'We have to go back the way we came.'

Marianne shakes her head, so slightly I think I've imagined it. 'We could be killed. Everyone will have real bullets this time.'

I feel sick to my stomach at the thought of being anywhere near the trenches, but we're out of options.

'It will not be that difficult.' Luc helps roll the fabric onto the tabletop. 'We can easily get our hands on some uniforms so we can look the part. Then we –'

'– Stop it.' Marianne says.

'– fall in line with the next regiment that comes past.'

My stomach is roiling. Thank goodness for all the noise in here, nobody can overhear us.

Mari glares at him, 'How can you even think like that?'

OK, we could have a problem. Sure, people can't hear us, but they can see the emotional daggers Mari's throwing Luc's way. 'Careful, we have an audience,' I mutter to them.

Something tics in his jaw. 'Nothing else has worked.'

Ain't that the truth? I hate this feeling. Being out of control, never knowing if we'll ever get home. That must be why my thoughts keep betraying me and I think about staying. Because then it would be my choice to stay, right? I'd be in control again. I'd be safe.

No, I'd be a coward.

'Maybe we could stay,' Marianne says. 'We are doing all right, yes? We have jobs, somewhere to live, and food to eat. We are safe here. And then after the war we can invest on the stock market like you said.'

But we can't. 'This isn't our world, Mari. We don't know if we're on the winning side.'

Mari's jaw drops. 'So you think we should get ourselves killed?'

'Shh! Keep it down!' People are staring at us. Any minute now Valerie will come back in and want to know why production is slow. I'm depressed enough already; I don't need Valerie adding to it.

Luc tilts his head towards the storeroom and we pretend we're going back for more fabric. All eyes are on us as we drag Mari out with us. Way to be subtle!

Luc shuts the door behind us. 'You don't get it? The Germans in this world probably win. They could advance on us and take us prisoner and . . . I dunno, send us to a concentration camp or something.'

Really? 'I thought that didn't happen until the Second World War?'

'That would be the movies again,' Luc scoffs.

Mari shakes her head. 'I cannot go to war. I will . . . join a convent and then I will be safe.'

Machine-gun laughter flies out of Luc. 'Safe? We can't ever be safe until we get home.'

That's when it finally hits me. I've been playing it safe. We've been playing it safe. My whole life my parents have been smothering me with safety. And it isn't doing us a lick of good because sometimes there is no safety.

Is there a bucket in here? Because I need to throw up.

The door flies open and Valerie is standing there. 'Get back to work!'

A different Ingrid walks out of that storeroom. Something has snapped in my head. Everything feels fuzzy and strange. A metallic taste fills my mouth. Instead of the clank and thunk of the factory, all noise turns to static buzz. Somehow my legs hold me up for the next few hours until the bell goes for the end of our shift. It isn't until we're back in our dorm that I register the headache that must have been building all day. Time for some poppy tea then. The fireplace is cold ash, but I'm so desperate I might just chew the stuff straight from the tin like it's a jar of peanut butter.

'Go easy on that,' Luc says.

He shouldn't even be in here. I guess they turn a blind eye to him coming to a girls' room because he's Mari's brother.

'I'm getting a full-on thumper. Can't wait for the kettle to boil.'

'You know it's an opiate,' he says.

'A-whattie?'

'An opiate.' He smiles and shakes his head. 'Poppy seeds are from the opium poppy. Opium poppies make heroin.'

'And opium, I guess,' Mari says.

I drop my spoon. 'Holy crap!'

'Please do not blaspheme.' Mari hugs her knees into her body. Any minute now she'll start rocking.

Now that I think about it, sitting in the corner and rocking back and forth holds tremendous appeal.

'Well, excuse us, sister.' Luc rolls his eyes and makes a sign of the cross.

I put the lid back on the tin of poppy seeds, then start flicking the seeds out from between my teeth.

'Relax. You are hardly a drug user. Just try not to get hooked on it or anything,' Luc says.

'What else can I take for headaches?'

Luc shrugs. 'We could get a café au lait down the street.'

'At this time of night?'

'Oh, I suppose not. Tomorrow morning then?'

'Yeah, that sounds like a nice idea.'

A strange melancholy creeps in. Will this be our last moment of peace before we have to do the unthinkable?

– EIGHTEEN –

WE'VE been working so hard these last days, an extra two hours' work each shift, making blue trousers for the troops. Valerie said the overtime was to make up for lost productivity. I think she really wants to punish us. She can't accuse me of faking my miracle because then I'll accuse her of the same thing for Henri. We've come to some kind of silent 'don't ask, don't tell' arrangement.

The extra work has kept us so busy it's stopped me thinking non-stop about dying, so that has to be a plus. But I'm so freaking tired all the time, and wired, and squirrel-brained and forgetful and just damned tired. I wish I had my tablets so I could soften all the freaking noise. My psychologist once said it was like having all the apps open on my phone all at once, and they were all as important as each other so I had to keep track of everything, and I remember thinking, 'yes, that's exactly what it's like.'

She also said it's not my fault I get repetitive and have the same thoughts, or even say the same thing a few times. She said something about co-morbidity being common with children on the spectrum, at which point my mum threw her hands up and said, 'One diagnosis is enough, thank you very much.'

Mari nudges me in bed, but I'm already awake. Luc is here and he thinks we should have a proper breakfast. He's being super nice all of a sudden. Is breakfast some kind of last supper?

'Do we have any money?' When did Mari send the last lot to the Gaillards. Did we reach a pre-agreed limit or is she just sending them money for as long as we're here? I suppose every bit helps.

'Plenty.' Luc jangles the coins in his pocket. 'Let's get so buzzy on caffeine we fly back to the trenches.'

Can we not talk about trenches for five minutes?

'Wait for me,' Mari grabs a scarf she's made from fabric cut-offs.

They are not going to leave me here on my own, stuck with these horrible thoughts of trenches and death. I slump out of bed to find Luc staring at me. 'What?'

'You slept in your clothes again?'

'So what.' I reach for my coat.

'Sorry, I didn't mean that as a criticism. We'll feel better after breakfast.' He wraps an arm around each of us and gives us a bit of a shake. Like that's going to cheer us up.

Luc said sorry. An actual apology. I don't want to bang on about it in case he gets all defensive and bossy again. But also; breakthrough, right?

At the cafe, the three of us squish around a table for two. Whether by accident or design, Luc's calf is touching mine. What do I do now? Pull away or leave it? There I go, over-thinking everything.

Sitting in the sunshine, sipping milky coffee would be divine if not for all the smokers at the tables nearby. They are all old men. They look about fifty. So haggard!

Acrid puffs waft over us. Mari and I cough.

Luc looks at me. 'Your lips are all cracked. Are you

dehydrated?'

Self-consciously, I lick them. They felt rough and jagged and sting a bit as they dry in the cool wind.

'Have this.' His jaw ticks as he pours me a drink of water from the jug.

'Thanks.'

Marianne gives me a nudge under the table.

'What?'

'Nothing.' Mari smiles and looks to her brother.

Luc frowns.

Must be some kind of twin thing.

Luc looks towards the train station. We follow his line of sight and see about twenty soldiers stepping into a carriage. They have pale, shiny faces. Thin bodies. Clean, new uniforms with the new blue pants. Well, that's one thing in their favour then. They should at least make it into the trenches alive.

They are so young.

A lump forms in my throat. It's obvious why Luc is being so kind to us. This coffee is lovely but it needs more sugar. Sugar is my friend today.

Mari turns to me, then to Luc. Moisture fills her eyes. 'Can't we try some other way?'

'What other way is there, apart from the way we came?'

The waiter, another old man, brings our croissants. Of course there are only old men here. All the young ones are dying on the battlefields. The waiter gives Luc a puzzled look, then returns inside.

This looks really bad. To any old stranger, Luc appears much older than the soldiers over by the train. Yet he's sitting with two girls, eating pastries, while everyone else his age is risking his life to save the country.

The awful truth is this will not be the war to end all wars. Another is coming soon enough. Another generation of destruction, an angry storm rolling across Europe.

Plus the Pacific, on my home turf, but the details are fuzzy about that.

'Are you absolutely sure the battlefield is the only way?' I'm doubting myself now. Because when we realised we were in the wrong world, I felt ready to do this. But now I've had time to think about it, obsess about it really, I don't know if I can go through with it. But if we don't go, we're stuck, aren't we? We'll never get home and we'll die here. Our families will never see us again.

'It's how we got here,' Luc says. 'It's how we get home.'

'I think I'll be sick.' The colour drains from Mari's face.

'I'm gonna puke up a storm.' Why am I making jokes when I feel like crap?

'Storm is right,' Luc says, pointing at the approaching dark sky.

The sun vanishes and a chill seeps through my skin. Splots of rain fall about us. We drag our chairs under the awning and watch the dark clouds roll in. The rain falls harder. Wet bullets splatter the ground.

With a blast of steam, the train pulls out of the station. If the rain keeps up, those poor soldiers might catch their death of cold before they reach the end of the line. Just as fast as the storm moves in, it rolls over. Sunlight beams through gaps in the clouds, steaming the wet ground.

'That is so weird.' Marianne looks to the clouds moving in the sky. 'Like the rain is following them to the battlefields.'

'I think I've worked it out,' Luc says. 'How we get back. Properly this time. It's not just going back the way we came, but going back during a storm.'

'So if we don't get shot, we'll get hit by lightning instead?' Mari asks. Because battlefields on their own aren't dangerous enough, are they?

Luc scratches his face. 'Maybe wars work like storms. Positive and negative forces create lightning, maybe war is a build-up of negative and positive forces.'

I'm so tired I've lost all perspective. Wars being compared to storms could be total insanity or the most profound thing I've heard Luc say. 'You're saying there are positives to having a war?'

Luc shrugs. 'Plenty. Patriotism, nationalism, pride, bravery.'

OK. That's kind of true.

Luc warms to his theory. 'Now that I think about it, wars are just like storms. They build up, explode and then things calm down. Until the next one.'

Mari says, 'It did start raining just as we climbed over the top.'

'Right,' Luc says. 'Then we stepped in that puddle. Then we heard all the bullets flinging about and we kept our heads down. Then we fell over that –'

Marianne shivers. '–I do not want to talk about it.'

'Eh?' Why the sudden overreaction? Mari has shut down.

Keeping his voice low, Luc leans over to me. 'We saw a body.'

Revulsion ripples through me. And there I was thinking my ordeal was hideous. They clearly saw more than me on their way through time.

Quick, change the subject. 'By the way, has anyone worked out why so many people speak English?'

'Maybe they're being polite to you?' Luc says with a smile.

Something flips in my tummy. It's kind of nice.

'I have a theory,' Marianne says.

Achievement unlocked, I've distracted her from thinking about dead bodies. 'Go on.'

'Valerie let me borrow some of her books." She produces one from her bag. "I grabbed this one while I was there. It's a novel, set a few years ago, before the war broke out. It's about a group of French rebels trying to re-take Calais.'

'Re-take Calais?' Luc says, doing a double-take.

I've heard that name somewhere. 'Where is –?'

'– A city on the coast, in the north of France. England is just across the channel.'

'Thank you Luc, I was about to say that.' Marianne rolls her eyes. 'The fall of Calais was a huge event in French history. It marked the end of the Hundred Year War. In our world at any rate. But this book of Valerie's, is about a plot to kick the English out of France, once and for all.'

'You had a war that went for one hundred years?' I can barely believe it.

'One hundred and sixteen, actually.'

'The British *still* have Calais in this world?' Luc's eyes widen.

'It's crazy,' Mari agrees.

A light goes off in my brain. 'So that's why the road signs –'

'– Were in English.' Luc finishes for me.

'So I was right, I noticed things that were important.'

'Yes. I'm sorry I didn't listen. We were all a bit stressed,' Luc says.

I was right. I was right! As this fresh information swirls in my brain, who should stroll into view but Henri. Minus his mask of simplicity. 'Bonjour, storm children.'

The café staff and patrons cry out cheery greetings all at once:

'*Henri!*'

'*Allo!*'

'*Mon ami!*'

They babble on in French, but judging from the tone, every single person loves Henri. Like a celebrity, Henri strolls in to the cafe where they continue the warm welcome. Pats on the back, hugs, free food, coffee.

All the same, that familiar nagging sensation drags at my memory at the sight of Henri. He looks so different now he's in uniform. 'It's total B.S.'

Luc chokes on his croissant.

'So cynical, Ingrid. He has found God, and been rewarded,' Marianne says.

I've had enough. 'Give it a bone! You're telling me God looks after that liar? Meanwhile all those soldier on the train, who've done nothing wrong, are heading to their um –' I can't say the word.

'Yes, but . . . they will all go to heaven.'

I should be more respectful to people's beliefs but I'm too angry to be considerate. 'How can anyone know that?'

Mari's mouth drops open, before she shakes her head and says, 'If there is no hope for something better, why would anyone bother?'

I throw my hands up in frustration. 'If God gives you life, then why would you throw it away? You'd better hope for their sake you're right, because a lot of them are not coming back.' When did I get so angry and mouthy?

A tear streaks down Mari's face. I feel like crap for making her cry.

'You think they should refuse to go to war?' Luc asks.

'Yes!'

'But then they will lose their country and the enemies will win.' Luc's eyes drill holes in me. 'Is that what you want? If they refuse to fight, the enemy takes over. They could die anyway. Surely by going to fight, they are giving their lives so that others may live?'

He's cornered me, but I'm too angry to listen. 'War is wrong, end of story.'

'This from the country that called us 'cheese eating surrender monkeys',' Luc says.

'What?'

'That was America, Luc,' Mari corrects him. 'Ingrid's country is the one that doesn't believe in global warming.'

'Don't blame me for what my government does, I can't even vote yet.'

Henri walks out of the cafe and I find myself staring at him. I've got my angry up now, and there's no calming down. 'Hey Henri? Why are you so transformed all of a sudden, eh?'

He gives me a half-confused look, and for a second I think he's about to become half-wit Henri again. But no, I think he's just translating. 'It is sudden,' he says in his heavily accented English. 'But there is little time. Tomorrow morning will be the last train to the frontline.'

I wanted a fight, I didn't want to be confused into actually having a conversation. 'Whaddya talking about?'

He pauses, as if it brings him such glee to be the bearer of this news. 'The army will be cancelling the trains from this line, then they will rip up the tracks to stop the enemy from seizing them and using the supply lines to get closer to Paris.'

Luc fires off a stack of questions to Henri in French, and I lose all connection with the conversation.

Mari translates for me, but my pulse hammers so hard it's impossible to make sense of anything.

Only two facts manage to penetrate my brain.

Tomorrow morning is the last train.

If we want to get home, we have to be on it.

– NINETEEN –

THAT night after our work shift, it starts raining again. Distant thunder rumbles through the heavens. At least, I hope it's thunder. It could be cannons. Is the enemy advancing on us already? That's why Henri said they were ripping up the train line, so the *Bôche* can't use it to take a ride all the way to the middle of Paris.

We're in our dorm. Luc has the fire going for us and it's pumping out heat. Even so, we're wrapped in blankets as we sit around it. My body wants to shiver, but I can't really be that cold. It's supposed to be summer but the weather reminds me of Melbourne, where sunglasses and a raincoat are totally normal things to wear at the same time.

'I have been thinking about your war and storm theory,' Mari says. 'It makes a lot of sense. But what I do not understand is how this equates to time travel.'

Luc jams another chunk of wood into the fire. 'I think it must be some kind of meeting of opposing forces. Like, at any one time, there are hundreds of thunderstorms all over the globe, just as at any one time there could be dozens of wars. A build up of positive and negative. So anywhere in the world, there could be a build up of positive and negative energy creating time travel.'

Mari presses him for specifics. 'And you're sure the time travel . . . hole or whatever it is . . . will open up for us on the battlefield?'

Luc shrugs. 'Nothing else has worked.'

Mari stares at him. 'We are about to follow you blindly into a warzone! You had better know what you are talking about.'

'We?' My stomach folds in on itself. 'You were going to hide away in a convent. Now you're going along with it?' I can't believe Mari is agreeing with this.

'Because you are going along with it too Ingrid!' Marianne says.

'But that was before!' Before Marianne had said she was in. Because, this following-Luc-into-battle scheme is one of those all-or-nothing deals. Mari was my convenient handbrake making me look brave. Now she's in, I can't back out or I'll look like a coward. Who am I kidding, I am a coward!

All of a sudden I can't help appreciating how brave–maybe foolish as well–all those soldiers and nurses are to be heading right towards the epicentre of the conflict. They're not heading in to the storm to find a way home, they're heading in to kill or get killed. People who do that sort of thing must be crazy. Yeah. Crazy brave.

This is the problem with having too much time to think about things. It gives me time to think about it! I don't want to think about any of this, I just want to get it over with.

Luc swallows and I can't help being drawn towards his neck again. The lean muscles are really beautiful. 'We need uniforms. What are your sizes?'

I fidget under my blanket. 'Eight to ten now maybe?'

'You are about the same as me,' Marianne says. 'We will

need thirty-eights.'

Oh God. Oh God oh God oh God. We are really going to do this.

Luc looks at us in turn. 'Right then. We need to be in uniform so we can get on that train tomorrow morning. That means we need to raid the factory tonight.'

***

The cool evening air nips at my ears as we skulk around the factory. There are no streetlights to guide the way, only the soy-milk light of the waning moon. At least the rain had stopped.

Of course the front door is locked, so Mari and I follow Luc around to the side of the factory, testing every door along the way. All of them are locked too. We almost complete a full circuit of the building before I look up and see a louver window. I tap Luc on the shoulder and point to it. Can't help smiling. Who's got two thumbs and found us a way in? This girl.

With a tilt of his head, Luc says, 'Up you get.' He braces his palms together to make a step for me.

Here goes nothing. I put my foot in his hands and he hoists me higher. My leg is pressed against him for both my balance and his. I really should stop thinking about the number of times we've been inadvertently touching each other lately. It's making me crazy. Then again it's nicer to think about Luc than thinking about going to the trenches and being shot at. Right, concentrate on the job. I pull the sleeves of my cardigan down to protect my palms and nudge the lower pane of glass free. The screech of glass on metal digs into my ears.

'Shh,' Luc says.

'Can't help it.' The glass comes out and I hand it to Mari, then get set on the next one. Screech. Eech. Eech. The noise eats my brain as the glass comes away.

'That should do it,' Luc says. 'Right, hop down now and hoist me up, I will climb inside and come and open a door for you.'

'OK.' Without thinking, I put my hand on his shoulder to steady myself. Heat pours through me at the contact. Luc makes it worse by unlocking his hands and grabbing my waist as I slip down. Hang on, why didn't I just crawl through the open window while I was up there? Because my brain's not working properly, that's why.

Luc turns to Marianne, 'Help me up.'

She locks her fingers and Luc is up and out of sight with barely a sound.

Why didn't he get the glass panels out then? Was it so he could show off his strength in holding me up first? Boys eh? How do I ever figure them out?

The cool air weaves around us as we wait for Luc to open a door from the inside.

'Should we put the glass back?'

'Yes, once we get inside,' Mari says, picking up a panel. I collect the other one.

'Pssssst!'

Luc's silhouette calls to us from a doorway. My first break and enter. Hey kids, don't be like me, stay in school, LOL.

Inside, the factory is black as pitch. We leave the glass panels by the door and use our hands to guide us along the walls.

'We should have brought a torch,' Mari says.

'Hang on,' Luc stops in front of us and hunches over. There is a scratching sound before light fills the room.

'You had a lighter in your pocket the whole time?' Mari says.

'Sorry. In all the excitement, I forgot.'

We can walk faster with the flickering light, but not so fast because the flame will blow out. Down another hallway, we find the packaging room.

'Right, you two guard the door and tell me if anyone comes.'

Worry twists my gut. 'What if someone does come?'

'Warn me of course.' Luc walks in to the room, taking the light with him.

The two of us are on the other side of the door. It's futile to try and make anything out in the dark. All I can hear is my pulse thumping in my neck.

Mari says in a low voice, 'we have certainly added to our skill set. Cutting out fabric patterns, starting a laughter club and now burglary.'

'You should leave the sarcasm to Luc.'

'True, he does it better.'

'I would have thought you'd stop him from stealing. Isn't that against one of the Ten Commandments?' Dang, there goes my mouth, running away from me.

'It is. When we get home, I shall be in confession for a week. But for now we must do this. If we miss the train, there could be no other way to get to the battle. We may have to do things through the proper channels. Enlist, do the training, undergo a medical examination, then get expelled when they find out we are girls.'

'You have a point there.'

The light inside the room flickers out. Luc yelps in shock.

'Are you all right?' Mari whispers into the room.

'Burned myself,' Luc's voice is muffled.

Sounds like he's sucking his thumb. With everything plunged into darkness, I strain my ears to work out what's going on. Luc is crashing into things, judging by the muffled grunts and thumps.

Bright light suddenly shines into the gloom, blinding me. I nearly yelp in shock when I hear Valerie speak. 'Looking for something, *mon ami*?'

Peeking around the corner, I see our supervisor in

a dressing gown and slippers, holding a lantern. Oh *merde*! I want to smack myself for being so stupid. Valerie is always here. She probably lives at the factory.

'I –' Luc starts. But doesn't finish.

'Luc. Dear Luc, what are you doing here at this time of night?' Valerie sounds concerned. Almost kind.

Marianne puts her finger to her lips to indicate we must remain silent. I mouth back, 'yeah, I know.'

'I am taking uniforms.' Luc says.

Wow. That's ballsy!

'And why would you do that?' Valerie asks.

At which point I realise they're both talking in English, which is kind of crazy. Because Valerie knows Luc is properly French, and she only ever spoke English for my–oh. For my benefit. She knows I'm here. Game over.

'I need to join the battle. I may be tall for my age, but they will find out I am too young. I tried to enlist before, but they sent me home.' Luc says.

Silence stretches to snapping point.

'I see. Then why are you are taking three uniforms, when there is only one of you?'

'Um . . .'

Yep, she definitely knows we're here.

A victorious tone enters Valerie's voice. 'Perhaps they are for Marianne and Ingrid? Do they want to fight as well? Are they here with you?'

Heavy with defeat, I move to get up but Mari holds me back and mouths, 'No.'

Luc says, 'You have probably noticed they are unlike most girls around here.'

'They are unlike any girls I have ever met. They say the strangest things some times.'

'They want to protect and help France any way they can,' Luc says.

It's not a lie. We do want to help France, but not through some crazy sense of patriotism, especially not in my case.

Time stretches as we sit here, waiting to see how this will play out. I can't help peeking around the corner again to see what's going on. Valerie puts the lantern down and steps closer to Luc. Her face looks soft and kind as she puts a palm to his cheek. 'You are still a boy. You should not give your life before you have lived it.'

What? Is she making a move on him? Sure looks like it. Now she's leaning in for a kiss. Mari grabs my arm to hold me back. Of course I'm tense. At the last second, Luc turns his head and Valerie gets only his cheek. I'm ridiculously relieved. Other feelings skate pretty close to jealousy, but I don't want to examine that.

'I see,' Valerie steps back. She takes the scarf from her head, folds it and presses it into Luc's hand. 'Then take this. It has brought me a great deal of luck and kept me safe. May it bestow the blessing of safety upon you.'

'Valerie you don't have to–'

'–yes I do. If you want to fight for your country, who am I to stop you? I take it you'll be catching the train tomorrow? Henri tells me there will be a two hundred strong company arriving in the morning ahead of moving to the front. With so many, nobody will notice a few extra. Now take the uniforms and go, before I change my mind and call the police.'

'Thank you, Valerie,' Luc says.

As we leave, Valerie calls out, 'Leave the glass panels where they are. You'll wake the whole village putting them back in.'

And there I thought we'd been pretty quiet about it. Oh God, I just remembered what Valerie said about leaving the next day.

I'm not ready.

But ready or not, here we come.

Back in our dorm, we fold the uniforms into neat piles on the table ready for tomorrow. No point laying them on the end of our beds, the last thing we need is bed bugs getting into them and making us even more miserable than we need to be.

It's tomorrow.

It's tomorrow.

It's tomorrow!

If only the bugs were the worst of my problems. My pulse is racing so fast I'll have a heart attack. Maybe dying tonight will be better than what we might face tomorrow?

Luc fishes a pack out of his jacket pocket. Are they cigarettes?

'Anyone else too strung out to sleep?'

Oh, they're a pack of cards. 'Count me in.' Anything to take my mind of tomorrow will be perfect.

'What game? Blackjack? Poker?'

'Snap?' Mari says with a shrug. 'Saves having to think.'

She's right. The last thing I need now is anything that will make me think. Of anything.

'Sure, why not.' Luc shuffles like a croupier in Vegas.

Show off.

Mari pokes the last of the wood into the fire to keep us warm. Rain rattles on the iron roof above us. Nervous calm descends as we sit on the floor, cards in our hands. Taking turns, flipping the cards down, it's the perfect distraction. Flick, flick, flick, flick, the cards don't always land directly, some slide away. Doesn't matter, we're doing something to eat up the time so we don't have to think about tomorrow.

Jack, eight, seven, two, seven 'Snap!' My hand whacks down.

'Don't think so!' Luc peels my hand away, 'There's a two

between them.'

'Sorry, jumped the gun.' Oh, bad phrase Ingrid, bad phrase!

Mari starts us off again. Eight, four, ace, queen, nine, ace, two, card, card, card, card. We're slapping the cards down so fast I can hardly see them–wait, 'Snap!'

'Where?' Luc pulls my hand off.

'There, see, two tens, just under the King Mari put on top.'

'Oh yeah,' Luc takes the top card off and starts pushing the pile towards me.

'But it's not a snap,' Mari reaches for them.

'Hey, just because you missed it doesn't mean I can't take it.'

Mari's brow creases. 'No because if you lay a card on top before anyone snaps, it cancels the snap.'

'Wha-a-a-a-t? You're making that up.'

'Mari, stop cheating.' Luc says, 'Give Ingrid the cards.'

'Of course you take her side.' Mari pokes her tongue out like a spoiled child.

I poke mine right back, 'Sore loser.'

'It's just a game,' Luc says on a sigh.

All the same, I'm claiming the cards. I won them fair and square. Flick, flick, flick we lay our cards down lightning-fast.

'Snap!' Mari bangs her hand down so hard I jump.

'Where?' Luc goes to pull her hand away but she's too fast.

'There were two-twos. You were both too slow.' Mari shoves the cards underneath the short deck in her hands and shuffles immediately.

Luc shrugs and gets ready to start again.

'No way. You're cheating. We've already had three twos show up already, you can't claim another two.'

'You're a card counter are you?' Mari's expression shoots holes in me.

'No, but I remember them from trying to snap them before, and I saw another turn up just before.'

'You *are* a card counter! You're cheating!'

'Don't call me *Rain Man*, I'm not cheating!'

'Girls!' Luc's palms are up. 'Relax. Nobody called you *Rain Man*, whatever that means. It's just a game of cards.'

'I'm not playing with cheats.' Mari gets up and slumps off to bed, mumbling something about how unfair everything is. This is what non-stop fear and tension does to people. Mari's been so supportive and caring the whole time, now she's throwing the closest thing I've seen to a tantrum. She must be so strung out.

'It's the stress.' Luc shuffles the deck. 'Want to keep playing?'

'Nothing else to do.' The last thing I want to do is go to sleep, because I know I won't be able to.

A bell rings in the distance as Luc deals out the cards. I don't remember hearing it before. 'Is that a fire drill or something?' No, can't be, it's only a short ring with no follow up.

Luc shakes his head as he finishes dealing. 'Lights out.'

What does he mean by—our lights go out. How strange. I must have fallen asleep every night before that bell rang. Or maybe it's a new thing, because the enemy is getting closer and we can't be turning the lights on to guide them to us?

Only the glow of the fire gives us anything. 'You haven't noticed that bell before?'

'Nope. How come you've heard it?'

He makes a half shrug. 'Don't sleep much.'

So Luc is human after all. 'Do you mean you don't sleep much or you don't sleep at all?'

'Are you going to play?' He looks at the cards in my hand, then up to me, waiting for me to join in.

Flick, flick, flick. It's harder to see the cards by the firelight. Maybe I'll let Luc win anyway, or we'll play 'Go Fish' instead. 'You know, not sleeping isn't some kind of personal failing. We've all had a lot on our minds.'

Luc keeps flicking his cards down, not looking my way.

Five, King, King 'Snap!' My hand slams the pile. Who knew I could be so competitive? Luc's hand presses over mine. Either they're the slowest reflexes in the world or he's holding my hand deliberately. Looking up, I can't help holding my breath. He is so utterly gorgeous in the firelight.

From under the blanket comes Mari's muffled voice. 'Will you two kiss and get it over with already?'

I might die right now.

'She's got a point,' Luc says. His hand is still on mine.

'Yeah?' I can't even tell if I said it or only thought it. Not that my brain works much these d–

Lips press to mine. Omigod, omigod, Luc is kissing me! Am I kissing back enough? Am I doing this right? Oh, his eyes are shut; I'd better shut mine. Holy freaking crap this is amazing! Bellyflippingly wonderful.

It feels so good; warm and just the right amount of pressure. My breath staggers in my lungs. His hand comes to rest on my shoulder, then moves to the edge of my jaw and the angle is so perfect I'm going to melt. I want to touch him, I want my hands all over him. Shuffle, shuffle, I get my hand onto the back of his neck, electricity jolts through me.

I want this kiss to go on forever.

I give the slightest tug on his bottom lip–I read about doing that on a dating app–and he makes the sweetest groan and returns the favour.

Omigod I just felt some tongue.

Freaking awesome.

– TWENTY –

THE wool uniform itches my legs as we stand at the train platform. In the light of day I can't help feeling self-conscious and confused about kissing Luc last night. I mean, it was amazing, but now it's the next day, we're dressed in our soldier's uniforms and doing our best to blend in with a proper company of soldiers. He's keeping his distance from me and hardly looking my way.

Sure, kissing each other here is a definite no-no. But it would be nice if he could hold my hand or accidentally brush past me or something. Otherwise I might start thinking he regretted it.

I keep my head low, not making eye contact with the rest of the soldiers on the platform. The main reason being I don't want to look into their innocent faces and start screaming about how they should run away from this now, while they still can. But also, I'm scared they'll look at me and see a girl dressed in men's clothes. Two girls in fact, because Mari is right beside me.

Please let my stupid hair stay tight in this cap.

The real soldiers are smoking and telling jokes, as if this is nothing more than a camping trip. It's impossible not to cough with so much smoke. Gag-making stuff. But I won't deny them a few cigarettes if it makes them happy. Not when this could be their last day on earth.

Well, this earth anyway.

Sure, Luc, Mari and I might look patriotic, but we're not going to the battlefields to defend France. We're going there to find a way home. We're not brave, not like these real soldiers. They don't have an exit plan, do they? They're going to win the war or die trying. It churns my stomach to think how many of these boys will never go home.

So many young faces.

Dizziness takes hold. I lean against Mari as a wave of nausea charges up my throat. Unable to stop it, I hurl chunks over the side of the platform, onto the tracks below.

Luc thumps me on the back. 'Easy, brother!'

Wiping my mouth on my sleeve, I have to check if anyone else has noticed me 'making wafers' as Mari would say. They are too busy being brave, chugging their cigarettes and making jokes.

The train pulls in and I throw up again, but nothing comes out.

'Stay close to me,' Mari whispers as she helps me up the steps onto the train. How she hasn't puked is a miracle. Oh God, are we really doing this? I guess we are. I was so keen a few days ago, but now the moment is here, what if I turn into a complete gibbering idiot and ruin it all?

The answer comes to me. I can't ruin it. End of.

Everybody on the train smokes. I thought they'd but them out on the platform but they keep right on puffing, lighting a new one with the end of the old.

I suppose long-term health issues don't rate when you're up against machine guns. Coughing and spluttering, Mari leads us down the train corridor and into a booth with bench seats. This is a much nicer train than the one we had earlier. How generous of the army to shell out for better carriages before we die.

Nobody is smoking in this cabin, which is a huge relief. Luc opens the window for me and I shove my head out, like a dog in a car, gulping for air.

By the time I sit down, Mari is clutching a string of rosary beads, her head bent down in prayer.

'You puke, she prays,' Luc says with a shrug. 'Here, have a sweet.' He holds open a paper bag filled with boiled lollies.

'Thanks.' I don't mean to be greedy, but the rock I choose has three others stuck to it.

'That is good luck,' Luc winks.

It tastes of raspberries. The sweetness triggers my mouth to watering and I start slurping. For some bizarre reason I feel almost happy. Now if I could only switch my brain off I won't have to think about what's up ahead.

Steam and soot from the engine pour through the window, caking our skin.

'How come you're not being sick?' I ask Luc.

'Nothing left,' he says with a weak smile.

It's meant as a joke, but if I laugh I might end up crying. Or puking again.

Luc wraps his arms around my shoulder and gives me a gentle shake. 'We'll be OK. I'll take care of you.'

If only you could, Luc.

To add to our misery, Henri walks in looking like a poster boy for the war effort.

Immediately Luc removes his arm.

What the hell is Henri doing? He looks like a movie star. He's sure been a great actor, pretending to be a sandwich short of a picnic all this time.

'Hello my friends.'

Shock ricochets through me as he takes a seat next to

Mari.

Luc snorts contempt. 'What are you doing?

'My patriotic duty,' he says.

The world has officially gone insane.

'Spread your legs,' Henri says to me.

'Excuse me?'

'You are sitting like a girl. Uncross your legs and let your knees fall apart.'

Oh!

Sitting beside Henri, Mari ignores all of us as she rubs away at the beads and prays in a soft drone.

Henri looks at her. 'The Lord works in mysterious ways.'

Revulsion ripples inside me as the train pulls away. I chomp down on the hard lolly.

Henri smiles. 'The three of you are my lucky charms. This adventure of ours will soon be over . . . consigned to history, if you will.'

Prick.

'Do not concern yourselves that I will expose your secret. My survival depends on yours, so I shall make sure nothing happens to you.'

His little speech is far from reassuring. Confusing more like.

The train chugs on through the countryside, passing small towns and green fields. We stop in what looks like the middle of nowhere–just a dirt road beside the train tracks–more soldiers climb aboard. As we start off again, I notice a platform on the other side. It's packed with people fleeing to Paris. Luc offers me more boiled sweets. The next one is striped green and white. It's peppermint, exactly what I need. My breath must be pretty horrible with the way my stomach is churning.

There are fewer buildings beside the tracks now. A smattering of trees with new, bright green growth of summer. The odd farmhouse. Empty fields. Hardly any people or livestock. Broken and abandoned buildings come into view. Half-trees. Cottages with their roofs blown off. Missing windows. Missing walls. Fields give way to churned paddocks with piles of mud and deep gouges of slop.

Great craters in the ground beside the railway tracks.

It looks like a war zone all right.

Luc holds out his bag of candy again.

'Is my breath still horrible?'

'A little,' he gives me a wink.

This new rock tastes like butterscotch. It soothes my throat and gives me another idea. In my satchel is the rest of the poppy tea. I unravel the tightly folded paper bag, lick my finger and dip it in the seeds. They are crunchy and get stuck between my teeth. After a while my tongue is pleasantly numb. The loss of feeling eventually moves down my throat and neck. It might just help me face the unimaginable terror that lies waiting for me in the battlefields. I fold the bag closed and slip it into one of my front pockets, within easy reach for next time.

Brakes screech in our ears. The train lurches violently and I'm thrown against Marianne. She stops praying to gasp in shock.

An explosion rips through the air. Shards of wood splinter the carriage. Fear chills me as we huddle together, yes, even with Henri, making ourselves as small as possible.

Another explosion rips the world apart. I scream but nothing comes out. At this rate, we'll be dead before we reach the trenches.

'*Venez! Suivez-moi!*' Somebody yells.

They're ordering us to move out, but I'm frozen rigid on the floor, looking at the world through my fingers. The walls between the carriage booths have blown away. There's a man in a red cap crawling up the aisle, checking each lifeless body along the way. His dismayed expression shows the futility of the situation. Shaking his head at the carnage, the red-cap peels the weapons out of their dead hands and gives them over to the living.

Red-cap sees the four of us huddled together. '*Qui êtes-vous?*'

Henri answers for us, his words coming out in a rush. I have no idea what he's saying. My ears buzz and whine as if another bomb is about to drop on us again. Thunder cracks the sky. Or is it cannon fire?

A swarm of hornets with megaphones drone overhead, followed by an almighty explosion.

Luc wrenches my hand; we're crawling behind the red-cap. Where is Mari? There is so much smoke and noise I have no idea what's going on. Just that I have to stay with Luc.

A hand grabs my ankle. 'It's me,' Mari says. 'Henri is behind me.'

We huddle with a group of boy soldiers. Playtime is over. This is all too real.

Somebody is handing out helmets which we're supposed to put on, but if I take my cap off, all that red crazy hair is going to come flying out and give the game away.

A shrill whistle blows out my eardrums and we scramble out the back door of the carriage, down a side ladder, using the train wheels to shield us from whoever is trying to blow our heads off. Smoke, dust, and the acrid stench of gunpowder fill the air. People are coughing and gasping. Other, more ghastly body smells assail my senses as Luc, Mari and I keep our heads down.

In the sky, planes dart and swoop. The soldier in the front seat is physically dropping a bomb out the front of the plane. It lands just the other side of the field, ripping the earth apart.

The screams. Dear God the screams are horrible. Gargling, choking, terrified screams. If I had anything left in me I'd be sick again. My stomach cramps on nothingness, my body trembles all over. I should have eaten the whole bag of poppy seeds. Not bothering to ask first, I dig my hand into Luc's pocket and grab another candy. Paper is stuck to it but I don't care. I need the sugar rush.

Gunfire peppers the air. The three of us flinch and duck our heads. I'm so scared, I think I've just peed my pants. Another blast of the whistle has us crouching and shuffling onwards, following the red-cap along the muddy ground until we find another group of shell-shocked soldiers.

That droning sound is back, and another bomb rips through us. Lightning burns my retinas, thunder shakes us to the ground. Heavy rain whacks our heads. It's impossible to steady my breath as we shelter behind piles of dirt. The red-cap signals, we have to move again. My ears don't work and my legs aren't listening because they don't want to move. We're on our hands and knees, crawling through the mud as rain attacks us from above. The ground angles sharply down; slip, splat, we slide into a deep trench. At least we're not out in the open any more. Maybe if I dig a cave, I can hide in there until the war is over.

Hang on. It doesn't make sense that the train line goes all the way to the battlefields. My stomach cramps again and I turn to Luc. 'We didn't reach Amiens, did we?'

His face is pale. Good, he's just as scared as me. Except that's bad, isn't it? He's supposed to be the strong one. He can't fall apart while I'm falling apart.

Huddling beside us, Marianne kisses her rosary beads, then wraps them around her neck. She grabs Luc's arm. '*Je suis prêt pour le combat.*' Next, she turns and embraces me, kissing both cheeks. I have no idea what she said, she forgot to translate for me. When bullets are whizzing over your head, conjugating verbs takes a back seat.

Hard rain makes everything slippery. The red-cap stays hunched down as he leads us through the trench. We reach a section where ladders line the walls. The noise of his whistle cuts a hole in my head, then he barks out orders. What's he doing?

The soldiers around us load their rifles and stand ready to climb the trench wall.

We're doing this now? But we only just got here!

Luc's gaze locks on mine. A strange quiet comes over me, making me feel lighter, somehow at peace. In stark contrast to the screaming and acrid smells around us. The cramping fear in my belly subsides, something soft and strange takes over. Maybe I'm already dead? Something tugs at my waist. I look down to see Luc tying a rope onto my belt loops. Then he ties it to Mari, then himself.

We're all in this together.

The red-cap blows his whistle again. The soldiers start climbing up. Machine gun fire fills the air. Luc touches his palm to my cheek. His face is closer. I nod. I want this. Do I close my eyes? Do I leave them open? Maybe he's just trying to talk to me and I'm completely misreading this –

His lips press on mine. The contact is soft but heat burns through me. Something clamps low in my tummy and I like it. It's way better than last night, so tender and sweet and an oasis of calm in a world or crazy.

His lips part on a breath. These are dizzy kisses. My heartbeat staggers behind my ribs.The outside world doesn't stand a chance of getting through, this kiss is everything.

Cannon blasts shake the ground.

All too soon Luc pulls away, his expression pale and vulnerable. Strange that it takes our imminent deaths for him to show his feelings.

Desperate for something to say, I blurt out, 'It's OK, I'm scared out of my mind too.'

'I am not scared.' But his expression betrays him as his mouth creases down at the corners.

Why else would he kiss me right now? Unless he thinks we're going to die and he's only kissing me because I'm the closest girl to hand and I really should stop over-thinking these things. Someone's yelling at us. Luc steps back.

It's the red-cap. He's shouting so fast I can't make it out. His face is purple. That can't be good. Neither is the gun he's pointing at us.

Thump! Henri appears out of nowhere and punches the red-cap hard in the side of the face. The officer falls like a lump of wood into a puddle, splattering us with a fresh coat of mud.

Henri. I'd forgotten all about him.

'*Aller!*' Henri says, grabbing the red-cap's gun for himself. 'Go!'

Crazy mixed feelings spread through me. Henri has saved us, but for what? So we can charge into battle and get shot to bits? Luc grabs me for another hug, and whispers in my ear, 'Keep your head down.' Then he kisses me again, harder, more passionate, making my heart hammer against my ribs.

Oh God. This is horrible. He's kissing me because he thinks we're all going to die? How dare he use me like that.

Even though I like it.

Luc turns, grabs the ladder and is gone. Mari quickly kisses me on both cheeks and follows Luc as the rope between them stretches taught. With a sob in my throat, I have no option but to follow.

Oh God, I'm going to die.

My legs don't work. I can't climb. The rope pulls at my

middle. Henri's hand is on my bottom, pushing me up and over. Is he in a hurry to see me killed? I'd kick him in the head if I weren't shaking so much.

With a shove from behind I'm out of the trench and into a world gone to hell. Where are Mari and Luc? There's nothing to see through the rain, smoke and exploding bombs. The tug of the rope tells me Luc must be ahead, dragging me. The ground rumbles from cannon fire and the storm overhead. Lightning splits the sky. Or maybe it's gunfire. I lurch forward, keeping lower than a snake. Every instinct tells me to get the hell out of here. Somewhere safe–preferably back in the trench. Back in Paris would be even better. Then I'll get a train to Switzerland or something and wait the war out.

Luc and Mari pull me along. The smoke clears, I see Luc's mud-splattered face. He's smiling at me. You bastard. How dare you enjoy this!

Overhead, one of those planes dive-bombs; they're so close I can see the airman in the front seat, about to drop something right on our heads.

"Duck!" I scream, pulling the rope away from the plane, dragging Luc and Marianne with me in a tangle of bodies and mud. Crawling forward, the three of us roll downhill into a crater. It's marginally safer than being out in the open. There's a puddle at our feet. A dollop of mud falls in the centre, making ripples. Something explodes inside my head and the ground falls away from me.

I am falling. Falling and weightless and yet somehow safe.

A hand locks around my ankle as everything turns dark. Am I injured again? Is someone dragging me off the battlefield?

Am I dead?

Eerie calm blankets me. My ears ring with the silence.

Oomph! I land hard on the ground, jarring my shoulder

and biffing my head.

Definitely not dead then, judging by the pain.

Looking up, the world is filled with blue sky and wispy clouds.

And the blessed white noise of silence.

In the next heartbeat, Luc comes into focus, a wild grin on his face. The sun shines behind his head like a halo. He kisses me, then grabs me into an embrace, knocking the wind out of me.

Rubbing my head, I pull back, looking from Luc to Mari. 'It worked!' The words come out as a laugh.

Marianne giggles and squishes us into a three-way hug. '*Merci Dieu.*' Thank you God.

We hug and giggle and kiss each other with relief. I can't stop laughing and crying at the same time. I'm relieved and excited and exhausted and . . . I don't know what. I kiss Luc a few more times than Mari. Not that I'm counting. OK, I am counting. Seven to three. She gets the cheeks, he gets the lips. Obviously.

Tearstains make rivers through Mari's muddy cheeks. Luc rubs his face as if he's only just keeping himself together. Mari unties the rope that binds us.

The sun warms my head. Fresh birdsong fills my ears. The trees are full of heavy green boughs that rock in the gentle wind. Across the grassy fields, men dressed in French and German World War One uniforms shake hands, smile in friendship and swig bottles of sports drinks.

We're back in the re-enactment, back where it all began. It's so peaceful and pretty. A veritable Eden compared to the maelstrom we've come through.

A strange thought crosses my mind. What if this isn't the re-enactment? What if we have all died and there really is a heaven? In which case, I owe Marianne a huge apology.

'*Félicitations, enfants de la tempête.*' I could have sworn that sounded like–

Henri.

Deep chills gnaw my stomach. Henri is sitting mere feet away.

I hate that smirk.

Luc grabs my hand.

Henri keeps right on gloating. His lips spread into a wild lottery-winner smile. He blinks a few times. '*C'est incroyable!*' His eyebrows shoot upwards as if he can't believe his luck. Above us, a commercial jetliner makes white contrails in the sky. Henri looks up to the aircraft and grins. '*J'appartiens ici.*'

I turn to Luc. 'What did he say?'

Before Luc can translate, Henri answers in perfect English. 'I said, 'I belong here' because I should be here.' Then he looks to the skies again, 'Such a shame Concorde no longer fly. They were fabulous.'

Not even a hint of worry about him. If anything, he's making a scrunched face as if I'm the stupid one.

Memories of Henri's actions come tumbling back. The way he'd been so interested in us from the moment we arrived at the factory. 'You weren't trying to save us in the storm, were you? You knew we were trying to get home, and you were after a free ride.'

'It feels so good to be back.' He puts his hand into his jacket and reaches for something. For a second I think it might be a gun. No. It's folded red fabric. He pops it open and puts it on his head.

A red kepi.

'I may have played dumb, but I wasn't so stupid to wear this on my head in the real thing,' he says. He gives us a broad smile that sinks holes in my stomach.

I bloody knew it, we had met him before. He was the

cheerful red-cap we met in the trenches, way back when this was all supposed to be make believe. Henri's been playing us all this time. My lips press together in anger. I want to strangle the smarmy prat.

'How long were you . . . away?' Luc asks.

'The best part of two years,' he says, dusting himself off. 'And you?'

Luc scrunches his face. 'A few months maybe?'

Jeez, Luc, stop chatting to him like we're friends.

Henri absorbs this information. 'Did anyone else travel like us? I saw none from our time but the three of you.'

One side of my head feels achy, like I'm coming down with a cold or something. It's behind my cheek and under my eye, making my face heavy and lopsided. I don't know if I can hang out until we get to a modern chemist. I want to get home and take a tablet so I can shut all the noise and confusion off. One more dip of poppy seeds, then I'll be fine.

Mari pipes up. 'What about Valerie? Have you left her to fend for herself?'

Henri doesn't look the least bit worried. 'Valerie will be comfortable and safe. I have seen to it she has everything she could want. A successful business with modern comforts.'

Standing up, Henri waves his arms above his head and cheers towards a larger group of pretend soldiers. 'Group photo time!'

There is no possible way I could be any more confused and irritated. What does Henri think he's doing? As we get to our feet, Luc leans towards me. 'I can't stomach this. He's acting as if this is all perfectly normal.'

I'm done with this. I don't think I have it in me to focus on any more problems. And my head has turned into a proper face-ache, as Mum would say. I miss Mum so much.

A few paces away, Henri approaches another group of re-enactment soldiers. They don't look the slightest bit fussed. They must have been here all the time, playing their war games. Having fun, unlike us. Sunlight glints off their helmets. Their rubber bayonets wobble on the end of their rifles. They chat to Henri, shaking hands and tripping over their tongues to thank him.

'*Merci*'

'*–Jour historique–*'

'*–Merci beaucoup–*'

'*–Excitante.*'

My stomach drops away at the sight of him getting so chummy with the soldiers. A photographer takes loads of shots, then points his camera at us. The ground suddenly looks really interesting. I don't want to be in any pictures. Henri turns away from the group and walks back to us. It gets the photographer focusing on us so I force a smile and hope it's over with quickly.

'So, children. The others seem to have enjoyed their adventure. Did you?'

'What sort of adventure did they have?' Luc asks.

'Oh, nothing like yours!' Henri says, slapping Luc on the back. 'I can't tell you how pleased I am. I have waited so long and now, thanks to the three of you, it's all finally working.' His voice drops lower. 'The four of us have achieved an amazing breakthrough for science.'

The happier he looks, the worse I feel. 'I'm not your lab rat!'

How dare he use us for an experiment!

– TWENTY-ONE –

SOLDIERS are shaking hands, laughing, patting each other on the back. The 'dead' rise from the ground and dust themselves off. They're all walking towards Henri, who in turn is leading the charge to the catering tent.

The three of us are wobbly and woozy from our trip through time. Sarcasm is my comfort zone. 'The war was fully catered, don't you know?'

Luc and Mari semi-laugh for my benefit.

The wait-staff are all wearing clothes of the era as well. Black and white penguin suits for the men, starched aprons and lacy caps for the women. On offer are bottles of mineral water and a full spread of nommable sandwich triangles. Chopped dates and nuts, egg salad, thinly sliced roast beef and tomato. I'm not letting the waiter move until I sample everything. Mari and Luc match me, bite for bite. The chicken with dill mayonnaise is my favourite so far, but the carrot and raisin looks yummy too.

'*Salut!*' One of the soldiers calls out. '*Vive l'histoire!*'

We look up, mid-bite, to see the host they're saluting is Henri. The food turns dry in my mouth.

'*Bienfaiteur!*' The soldier calls out, holding his flute of sparkling wine. It's probably proper champagne, considering where we are. The way my head is spinning, I'd best stick with mineral water. I whisper to Luc, 'Been-whatter?'

'Benefactor. I think . . . oh *merde*. They're thanking him because he paid for the whole re-enactment.'

If I don't find a seat in the next second my knees will give way. I stagger to a folding chair and practically fall into it. I feel horribly used and . . . yes, violated. It's one thing for Henri to want to bring history back to life, but he took a massive liberty dragging us along with him. We could have been killed! Then another admission of failure worms into my brain; we were so preoccupied with our time problems, we didn't notice what Henri was really up to.

'Breathe.' Mari rubs my back. 'We're all OK. Everything will be fine now.'

Hot and cold flushes race through my body. Those delicious sandwiches will make am encore if I don't control myself.

Also, Henri must be minted to be able to afford all of this.

'Sweet girl, is it all too much?' It's Henri's voice, and he's speaking English. Can't be for anyone's benefit but mine. 'What happened to you my dear?'

Mari does the talking, but with all the buzzing in my ears they may as well be speaking Swahili. I've over-clocked my brain; reached the point where I've taken too much in and I can't process one more thing. Sitting still makes me dizzy.

'Water,' I croak out. Oh man, I am such an idiot. I'm dehydrated. That has to be it. All the throwing up and sweating and falling through time and then straight into the smorgasbord of sandwiches. This is so embarrassing. 'I'm OK. Thanks. I just need a drink.'

Fsssssht Luc twists open a bottle of sparkling mineral water and holds it for me, making sure I have a good grip. The bubbles tickle my throat but they don't slow me down. Someone else brings a bottle of sports drink and I grab that, chasing the mineral water. 'I'm so sorry,' I can't help apologizing. Everyone must be looking at me.

'Don't be,' Mari says, helping herself to a sports drink as well. 'I'd say we're all worn out.'

Henri looks into my face. 'Please visit the medical tent, just to make sure.'

It's good advice, but because it's from Henri I don't want to do it.

On the other hand, Luc and Mari also think it's sensible. Before I can protest, they have me on my feet, supporting me from each side. It's a bit of a stretch to call it a medical tent. There's a first aid kit and an army bed that could be from nineteen sixteen. After another guzzle of modern-day sports drink, I'm starting to feel human again. Any other day I'd be busting for the toilet by now. Shows how dried out I've become.

'Everything is going to be OK,' Luc says, taking a sip from his own bottle. 'We made it back, and we're all in one piece.'

'No thanks to Henri,' Mari says.

'Got that right.' I nod to her. 'I want to clean his clock.'

'Pardon?' Mari makes her confused face.

It's something my dad says, when he's trying his best to sound Australian. 'Sort him out. Pay him back for everything he's done to us.'

'That's not a very nice thought.' She looks disappointed in me.

'I'm not in a particularly *nice* mood. You can't just suck people back in time and say it's for science, like some cosmic get-out-of-jail-free card. The man as good as kidnapped us.'

Luc butts in, 'Good luck explaining that to anyone.'

'All sorted now, children?' Henri walks in to the tent and closes the flap behind him. What's he doing bothering us again? 'You were amazing,' he grabs Luc by the hand and gives it a vigorous shake.

'No thanks to you!' It's hard to be in a forgiving mood with everything he's put us through.

'I did my utmost to protect you, every step of the way,' Henri says. His expression virtually dancing with excitement. Of course it is; he's made an incredible scientific breakthrough.

'Why did you have to drag us into it?' *Ungrateful* stacks on top of my list of emotions. If he'd asked us if we'd wanted to travel through time, Luc probably would have volunteered. But I wouldn't have, that's for sure. Or at least, I'd have had a chance to think about it. What am I thinking? I would have said no. Definitely.

Henri smiles at us. 'You are right. I should have asked permission.' Is that an apology? He hands us his business card. 'If you ever want to do this again, let me know.'

'You've got to be bonkers!' I blurt out. 'Do all that again. No way?'

'Oh but we must!' He clasps his hands together. 'For this to be scientifically valid, we must replicate the experiment and achieve the same results!'

Mari says something in a low tone. It sounds like some good swears. I must get her to teach them to me. She grabs my hand and yanks me to my feet. 'We're going. Come on Luc.'

Luc is a bit slower, stopping to take Henri's card on the way.

Mari snatches it out of his hand, throws it to the ground and stomps on it. She glares at Henri 'One day, Monsieur, you will pay for what you've done to us!'

Good one, Mari!

Henri pushes home his point. 'Don't be angry. This is a time for celebrating.'

'Celebrating the fact we are still alive, through sheer luck rather than planning.'

Thank you Mari, that's exactly what I was thinking.

'Which is exactly why we need to do this again,' Henri says. 'Out of this entire re-enactment, with the conditions perfect, you three were the only ones to take such a journey. We must investigate further.'

'–!' I can't even make a sound. Neither can Mari. Luc's eyebrows jolt northwards, then come crashing down in confusion.

'Once is happenstance,' Henri says. 'Twice makes the pattern. Three times confirms it all. This is such an exciting discovery, it must be confirmed. Yet we have so many unanswered questions. Such as why we all left at the same time, yet I travelled further into the past than yourselves? My theory is that being on my own threw me further back, while you three were together so didn't travel so far. A weight versus distance ratio, only in this case, time is distance. We would need to do it again to confirm my hypothesis. What are you doing next Saturday?'

My ears ring loudly with fury.

Luc shakes his head. 'I'm sure I speak for the girls when I say we've had enough experiments, *merci*.'

'But we have only just begun! Think of the mysteries we can unravel. Working together, we would make history!'

Anger speaks for me. 'Or get shot in the head. No thanks!' I take Mari's hand in mine and together we storm out. The tent has no doors to slam. The canvas flap doesn't have anywhere near the impact. Hang on a second. Luc hasn't come out with us. If I go back in the tent, I'll ruin our dramatic exit. 'Luc, stop mucking about.' I'm torn between walking away and going back in to drag him out of there.

Mari tugs at my hand. 'Come on. If Henri's paying for this, the least we can do is eat all his food.'

Good idea, even though I'm not hungry any more. We can wrap a few sandwiches in serviettes and take them home with us. I could probably fit a few bottles of sports drink in my backpack too.

There are loads of soldiers in the catering tent, talking, laughing, eating and drinking. The serving trays are groaning with food. Nobody's going to care if we take a few extras.

'Here you are.' Luc catches up with us as we're wrapping our 'later-ons'.

'You took your time.' Even to my ears I sound catty.

'Fair call. Henri's something else, isn't he?'

'Did you punch him in the throat for me?'

Luc snorts a laugh and I start laughing with him. But somehow it comes out as a choked sob. Before I can stop, fresh tears spring out. Suddenly I'm bawling my eyes out.

Luc grabs me in a hug. 'It's OK Ingrid, everything is OK.' I'm not sure if he's doing this for my comfort or to hide my face from everyone else. This is so embarrassing. People are coming up and asking questions. I'm not exactly sure what they're saying but they sound concerned.

'Time to go,' Luc says for my benefit. He wraps his arm around my shoulder and leads me out into the grassy fields.

I never thought I was such a cry baby but I can't stop. It makes no sense. I'm not in danger any more. We're safely back in our own time. In our own world. Why cry now?

'What happened back there?' Luc asks me.

'I don't know.' I wipe my face on my coat sleeve. Ow! Forgot there were buttons on the cuffs. 'I don't think I can stop.' Come on tears, dry up. But they won't. If anything, they're getting worse. My knees give way. I fall into the soft grass. My whole body is shaking.

'Let it out.' Mari crouches beside me and wraps her arms around my shoulders. 'We've had a huge day. Correction, we've had a huge couple of months. I think we are exhausted.'

Of course! It's exhaustion. Now that I know why I'm such an emotional basket case, I feel so much better. The tears dry. I look up to Mari and Luc. 'Can we go home, please?'

– TWENTY-TWO –

BEING home with the Durand family feels alien, as if I'm still time travelling. Everything familiar is new and wondrous. Cars are a thing of beauty, the television in the corner is a magic portal. The natty old couch is the most comfortable furniture in the world. We've been away so long, but as far as we can tell, in real time it happened in one afternoon. Nobody apart from Henri knows what we've been through. Nobody else would understand.

Luc and Marianne's mother fusses over us as we return, making big hand gestures for my benefit as she talks a mile a minute. Mari hugs her mother too hard, and she expresses surprise at the emotional outpouring, but hugs her daughter anyway.

We stink and we're covered in dirt. I'm desperate to get clean, but it's a one-bathroom house and I'd love nothing more than a super long, hot shower. Luc and Mari need one too so I can't waste time. It feels so good to wash my hair and slather conditioner through it. The simple act of wearing normal clothes again is pure bliss. I check the clock and calculate the time zones. Hah, more time troubles. It's doing my head in. It will be far too early in the morning in Melbourne. I just want to hear Mum's voice, but if I call her now she will think something terrible has happened. Something terrible *has* happened, but I can't tell her. In any case, from Mum and Dad's perspective, they spoke to me only a couple of days ago.

The tablets by my bedside call to me. But it's late afternoon. Nearly the evening. If I take one now, it will keep me awake all night. So I have to wait until the morning. Until after I've eaten some food. Screw that, I need one now. After everything we've been through, there's no way I'll sleep tonight anyway. I have to shut the noise out and get some freaking peace and quiet.

Marianne comes into the bedroom we share, drying her hair with a towel. 'I think we are in for some big adjustments.'

'I won't miss the bugs, that's for sure.' My bed feels like a warm hug. I could sleep for a week. I can't help wondering if Luc will come in and chat, like he used to, in our dorm back in nineteen sixteen. Will he go back to ignoring us? Don't judge me, but I wouldn't mind some more kisses. I really hope that when he kissed me, they weren't pity kisses. Especially the kisses in the trenches. Were they a kiss before dying? Now we're not dead, he'd better not pretend they never happened.

He won't be that horrible, will he?

Oh dear, there he is standing in the doorway.

'Mari, *mère* wants you.'

That's funny, I hadn't heard their mother calling.

'Sure she does,' Mari rolls her eyes and makes a smirk as she gets up. 'I will leave the two of you alone.'

Flip. There goes my tummy. Luc walks in and sits on the opposite bed. This could end either in awkward silence or me jumping him.

'Are you feeling better?'

'A bit,' I haven't processed everything. I'm not sure I'm

ready to. 'The shower helped.'

'It sure did. I smelled like a dead skunk.'

'You weren't that bad.'

He smiles and shakes his head and we're back to stretching the silence again. You know how sometimes people can be together and not talk and still feel comfortable? This is the opposite of that.

Luc softly clears his throat. 'Ingrid, I am sorry for kissing you.'

'Oh come on! Don't apologize for it.' Why can't I say something clever? Instead I sound offended. I am offended. And embarrassed as hell because obviously I did read way too much into it.

'Let me explain,' Luc puts his palms up in a sign of peace. 'I promised my parents, because they promised your parents, that I would look after you and treat you like a sister and . . . not take advantage of you.'

I want to die. Now please.

'But, obviously that didn't happen,' Luc says, moving from Mari's bed to sit beside me on mine.

OK, maybe I don't want to die any more. 'I kind of had to promise the same thing to mine. Mum nearly cancelled the whole trip when she found out I'd be living with a boy.'

Luc smiles at me and takes my hand in his. Warmth spreads up my arm at the contact. 'They are right to worry about you. You're going to break hearts wherever you go.'

Heat radiates through my neck and cheeks. 'So are you.'

Here's the silence again as he keeps rubbing my hand and our gazes lock.

'I don't think I can treat you like a sister any more.'

'OK,' His confession makes me bold. 'You gonna hurry up and kiss me or what?'

'*Oui.*'

Oh yeah.

***

That night, the three of us are lazing about in front of the television. Doing very little is a huge source of comfort. There's a lot of pretending going on between Luc and me, we're sitting here pretending to watch television, when what we're really doing is holding hands, and my thumb is tracing shapes in Luc's palm.

An ad comes on for an upcoming memorial service for the fallen. Henri appears on screen. Seeing him makes me want to puke. He's wearing a dark, three-piece suit with a fob watch attached to it. Luc does all the translating. He's spouting something about honouring history. My pulse hammers so hard I can't take it in.

'I want to bury him in a trench,' Luc says.

'Stop it.' Mari slaps him on the arm.

'I like the way you're thinking, Luc.'

'Of course you'd say that,' Mari interrupts.

Why does seeing Henri bring out the worst in me? 'I just . . . I can't help wanting him to suffer for what he did to us.'

'Payback?' Luc raises an eyebrow.

'Nothing too horrible,' I back away from my previous thoughts of punching Henri's lights out. That might end up with assault charges and me being sent home. Not smart. 'I just want to . . . I don't know. Mess with his head. Or just . . . do *something*.'

The screen fills with fields of red poppies. So many thousands of soldiers died in that horrible war and Henri used their energy and patriotism and courage to fuel his time travel fantasies. Well, not fantasies any more. Because we really did it.

203

'Whoa! Poppies!' I blurt. 'They make opium, right?'

'Some poppies, but not those.' Luc shakes his head. 'They are totally harmless.'

Marianne twists her mouth. 'Nice idea though.'

Luc and I stare at her in shock. Mari puts her palms up. 'I'm not a saint. I wouldn't mind seeing Henri get what's coming to him either. Not that we stand a chance, I mean the man's filthy-rich-untouchable.'

OK trump card. 'You forget. I've still got the right sort of poppy seeds in my backpack. The ones Henri gave me from nineteen sixteen.'

Luc looks at me with such admiration I feel like I'm glowing from the inside and says, 'Maybe we can stitch him up.'

'Nothing too horrible,' Mari says.

'Perhaps a taste of his own medicine.' Luc draws out a dirt-stained business card from his back pocket. 'I can make a call to arrange a meeting.'

***

We're outside a dance party in a field on the outskirts of town.

'Are you sure this will work?' Marianne chews her bottom lip.

Luc takes a deep breath. 'We will find out soon enough.'

Trance music dush-dushes up the grassy hill. Psychedelic lights beam into the sky above the open-air rave. Towards the ticket office, police and sniffer dogs patrol everyone going in and coming out.

We can't be sure Henri will come. Deep down, I guess it's pure fantasy thinking we can do anything to him. I looked up Henri Ederle, he's stinking rich and owns a football team. We're just three kids he used for a science experiment.

'Those dogs can't smell us from here, can they?' Mari asks.

'I hope not.' Luc and I say together. Oh, we are so in synch.

What's really nice is that my tablet feels like it's working and I'm not distracted by every little noise, blade of grass, gust of wind. I can focus on the task, even with someone as distractingly gorgeous as Luc beside me.

'Where is he? Henri should have shown up by now.'

'Stop checking your watch.' Luc nudges my shoulder. 'He'll come.'

It feels like forever, but about ten minutes later, on the road below, a stretch limousine pulls up. The driver gets out and opens the rear passenger door. Henri strides out onto the path, looking like he owns the world. My mouth turns dust-dry as we walk towards him. He's so intimidating in a modern business suit. Hard to reconcile this Henri with the dopey labourer back at the uniform factory.

Luc nods to him and holds out the shopping bag. He speaks in English for my benefit. 'Valerie sends her best wishes.'

Henri's face remains impassive as he takes the bag. 'This is how we play it?'

'Look in the bag,' Luc says.

Henri makes that classic French shrug, as if he doesn't care one way or the other. My pulse charges as I watch him reach into the bag.

Go on. Take it out and hold it.

He lifts Valerie's scarf, caresses the fabric in his fingers for a second, then drops it back in the bag.

Damn! He's supposed to hold on to it. I swear my heart stops. What good is a scarf soaked in poppy tea if Henri doesn't have it close to him? How many times did we wash our hands and clothes afterwards to remove all traces of opiates? I still reckon the sniffer dogs will smell it on us.

'Where is she?' Henri says.

'In there.' Luc tilts his head towards the rave party. 'Last time we checked, she was getting a taste for it.'

Marianne's trembling hand reaches for mine as we take a few steps towards the party, hoping Henri and Luc will follow.

'You expect me to believe that?' Henri says. 'That you have gone back, without me, and retrieved Valerie . . . and now she loves the *discothèque*?'

I can't breathe. It's not going to work. The dance party and the police may as well be a mile away. Any moment now Henri will storm off in the wrong direction.

No, he heads the other way and blocks our path to the dance party. He points at Luc to emphasize his words. 'I played dumb once, but I'm not an idiot. This–' he reaches into the bag and pulls out the scarf, clutching it in his hand '–is not Valerie's. I know you did not go back and get her. She does not belong in this world. People cannot go forward, they can only go back and then return to their time of departure. It's how it's always worked.'

'Really?' I'm too fascinated to know when to shut up. 'But what if we'd tied another person to us as we came back. We could have brought them with us?'

Luc rubs his forehead.

'No.' Henri shakes his head. 'It does not work like that. It will never work like that. Believe me, I have tried.'

Me and my big mouth. I all but admit we're lying. It is Valerie's scarf though, it's the one she gave to Luc the night we stole the uniforms.

Then Henri does something wonderful. He puts the scarf around his neck and ties it like a cravat.

I can't breathe for excitement and fear.

'You are Satan himself,' Marianne says.

'We have resorted to name-calling?' Henri says.

Luc clears his throat. 'Valerie is in there. Go and see for yourself.'

'You are lying, and you are bad at it,' Henri says.

'Call my bluff then.'

I can't swallow.

Henri turns and sees the police. 'You know, I could have you three arrested for . . . oh, I will think of something. I just need to call them over and things will get very ugly.'

Yes please. That's exactly what we want to happen.

Luc starts shouting in French, as if he and Henri are having a heated argument. That gets the officers' attention. Two of them walk towards us, each with a harnessed Alsatian by their side. Obviously they're called Alsatians here, not German Shepherds.

'*Pathétique*,' Henri says.

Time moves insanely slowly. Henri takes two steps towards the police. The three of us take two steps back, as if we're scared of the dogs, or him.

Henri talks to the police in a calm tone. The dogs pull forward. I flinch, expecting the dogs to go crazy and maul him or something. Instead, they remain calm and sit beside him. Henri pats one of them on the head and strokes his ears as he keeps up the conversation.

'*Merde*! It hasn't worked. Let's get out of here before he sets them on us,' Luc says.

Defeat saps my strength as Luc leads me away. Turning back, we see the dogs still sitting there, their tails wagging. The police walk towards us, but the dogs won't budge.

Henri pats the other one. They bark in unison. The officers can't shift them.

'Luc, Marianne, stop for a second. I think it's worked. I think they can smell the poppies on him.'

Sure enough, the dogs refuse to move, making the police freshly interested. Victory fizzes through my body as more police walk towards Henri. The dogs stay put. The only way they can get the dogs to move is to make Henri move. Towards the drugs testing van outside the rave party.

'*Merci Dieu.*' Marianne drops to her knees.

'You can say that again.' I let out a long-held-in breath. Call me a horrible person, but there's something really satisfying about seeing Henri get into trouble. Considering all the trouble he's put us through, this is the least we can do.

Luc grabs me in a bear hug and swings me around. Light headed and giddy, I can't tell him to stop. I don't want him to either. Maybe I'll just have to kiss him again.

***

At breakfast the next morning, I'm determined to act as if everything is normal. But how can I with victory dancing in my head? Henri is getting his just desserts. Kissing Luc last night was pretty fabulous too.

'Good morning Ingrid,' Madame Durand greets me with a kiss on the cheek. 'I am making what you call French toast.'

'Yum, thanks!' I take my seat, nerves jangling. I want to dance and sing but only Luc and Marianne will understand why. They're all jangly after our success last night too, I can tell.

'Good morning Luc.' A silly grin takes hold. I suck at pokerface.

Luc chooses the seat beside me, sitting so close his leg touches mine. Warmth spreads through me.

Madame Durand brings me a plate of the fried eggy bread. The knowing look on her face tells me she's noticed something between Luc and I.

'Is there any tomato sauce?'

Madame Durand gives a sweet smile and fetches the bottle from the pantry. 'It is nearly empty. *Quel dommage.*'

'Can I try some of the Dijon mustard as well?'

Her face lights up as she hands over the jar.

Monsieur Durand turns up the volume on the television in the corner. 'Have you seen this? They arrested Henri Ederle on drug charges.'

'Wow,' Luc and I say together. If I look directly at Luc, I won't be able to keep a straight face.

Marianne walks in, half yawning. She moves to take her seat beside me and notices Luc in it instead. A smile spreads over her face and she turns it into an exaggerated yawn.

'This is Ingrid's recipe from Australia,' Madame Durand says as she serves more plates of breakfast.

I cut off a slice, dip it in tomato sauce then dab mustard on it. It tastes like magic and makes me heart-sore for home.

Monsieur Durand turns up the television volume. Henri's speaking to reporters, he's smiling and looking confident. Yeah, he'll get off. He's got plenty of lawyers and loads of money. Still, it's nice to know we've messed with his head. Not so much revenge that we've turned into horrible people ourselves, but enough to show him he can't use us for experiments and get away with it.

Something vibrates against my leg. It's my mobile phone going off. Happiness pours through me when I see Mum's face on the screen.

'Hey Ingrid. I miss you sweetheart.'

'I miss you too, Mum.'

'What did you get up to on the weekend?'

Luc moves into view. 'Hello Misses Calloway. We had a great time fighting the First World War. Ingrid was *tres bon.*'

'He's being silly,' I gently nudge Luc out of view. 'How are you?'

'I'm fine.' A tone of suspicion creeps into Mum's voice. 'Ingrid, do you want to tell me something.'

Heat roars up my neck. 'Muu-u-m!'

'Just asking.'

Marianne laughs out loud.

'Is everything all right?' Mum asks.

Madame Durand makes a pot of coffee, filling the kitchen with tantalizing aromas. Monsieur Durand switches off the news and tucks into his breakfast.

Luc keeps smiling at me.

It all fees so wonderfully ordinary and normal.

After everything we've been through, I could do with a dose of average for a while.

'Yeah, Mum. Everything is perfect. Everything is as normal as can be.'

***

You would have thought I'd never want to see a trench or a battlefield ever again, but you'd be wrong. We've taken an extra trip this afternoon to a place called *Main de Massiges*, a restored series of trenches from World War One, now a monument to the dead. The stark piles of rocks and dirt, sandbags, barricades and barbed wire look so familiar and real. The gentle breeze, warm sun, sturdy pine trees and crowds of tourists make it alien and unreal.

'How are you holding up?' Luc asks.

'*Bien,*' I say with a nonchalant shrug. I'm trying to use the local lingo.

'I love the way you mangle our language,' Luc gives me a squeeze.

I've been in France for months. I'd better have something more to show for it than, '*je suis Australien*'.

'Is this weird to you?' Luc asks.

'Beyond weird. But a good weird, you know?'

I had to come here. We had to come. Here we are, Luc, Mari and me, walking through the timber-lined trenches, my hand touching the dirt whenever I can, to earth me to the spot.

'You are not OK, are you?' Luc has a way of seeing right through my brave face.

'Nope.'

'Do you want to leave?'

Mari is a few steps behind us and says, 'We just got here.'

She's right. 'No, I don't want to leave.' I can get through this. It's not as if we're in a war any more. Just the memorial to the fallen.

He gives me another encouraging squeeze.

I can't help asking, 'What's French for *post traumatic stress disorder?*'

He says it so fast, I swear he just repeated my words, but with a French accent. Well, whatever the translation, I probably have a dose of it, but not as much as the real soldiers who faced real dangers in the real thing.

This wasn't the same spot where we fell through time and fought our way home, but there are so many battlefields like this all over the country. So many thousands and thousands of brave soldiers and nurses and helpers, volunteers and mercenaries on both sides. Stupid and optimistic and completely misled into being here.

But above that, far above that, they were so insanely

brave I can barely comprehend it. I've been through it,
but I didn't really get it. Not until now. Now I know
what they really went through.

Now I know, I am only just beginning to understand.

***

The End

One more thing . . .

If you enjoyed reading the book, please share your opinion with others and leave a review on your book-buying website of choice. Reviews are like oxygen for writers; they help spread word-of-mouth magic in an incredibly crowded marketplace.

To keep up-to-date with Ebony's book releases, events, giveaways, exclusive content and general shenanigans, please visit her website at www.ebonymckenna.com.

One MORE *more* thing:

Special Thanks . . .

Huge hugs and love to everyone who keeps relentlessly encouraging me to write, especially Alison, Clare, Carol, Denise, Louise and Sara from The Saturday Ladies' Bridge Club.